THE
PLACE
WHERE
BUILDINGS
GO

THE PLACE WHERE BUILDINGS GO

A Novella

CARRIE VRABEL

Permanent
Record Press

THE
PLACE
WHERE
BUILDINGS
GO

ONE

Today, most of Claypool, Indiana, is farmland that big agribusiness companies have invisibly purchased. What's left are rotting farmhouses that the families of old farmers and farmers' wives, either dead or in nursing homes, rent to men who want the space to shoot their rifles. There are tall, oddly shaped boys with shorts to their knees and a hundred flea bites, little red dots. And the night. And men moving out in it.

The land here has been made flat and plain, a place for trains to cross, carrying corn syrup and soybeans to people who don't know they're waiting for it, for thin trees to silhouette themselves against sunsets. Death sits on us bare like the day sits on the hill, like the night sits on the lake. And I guess the men manage their fear of waiting for it by hammering objects into the ground and inventing occupations, and the women push it away by convincing themselves that men know something they don't—that the work men do holds a truth that is the natural extension of a shelter logic, a logic that begets shelter.

Men split the world. The outside. The inside. And now the outside is as strange and unfamiliar as a dream.

My mother and I live with L and the cats, and with my grandmother, old Mary, in my father's house. He built it in 1975 with his friends and with some high school boys he hired. They smoked cigarettes and laid concrete. They drove big trucks that rolled heavy as boulders. They popped nails into naked wood.

When I was twelve, my father died. His tractor tire hit a sink hole in the field and rolled over with him on it. Now the three of us women, and L, and the cats, live in his house like it's the only shade tree in a bare field. But instead of the tree growing up out of the ground, my father pounded it down in, harder than you could imagine. And now Mary keeps her lace and porcelain figurines and tiny portrait of Jesus in it.

Out here, on cold mornings, there are trucks pulled over on both sides down 900 South. Like waiting to watch fireworks. But they are all men and boys. In each truck, one in the passenger, one in the driver's. They wait in heated cabs for a four-legged girl to emerge from the small square of woods in the middle of three hundred flat acres. There is a story that starts with cave paintings of stick men pointing arrows at figures with four stick legs. I think this is supposed to be a continuation of that.

At night the trains rumble so low it hurts my stomach. Heavy like looking down a well, like death asking me whether I'll have it today or another day. On County Farm Road, Tim drives his huge tractor with half-closed eyes, and everyone is so calm. Orderly. Trusting him to stop at the right places and not do something typical to get us all killed.

     THE PLACE WHERE BUILDINGS GO

Hunters marry their wives here. My mother married one in 1973. She was pin thin, which is why he asked her. I went to kindergarten with my generation of them. They rode the bus with camouflage backpacks, tucked-in Hanes undershirts, and boy-sized gold belt buckles. Paper bag lunches with grease spots already, even in the early morning. They could not spell and pushed each other off the tops of metal slides and did things to insects and worms that made their hands smell sick. Now, my mother and I call them the killing men.

TWO

I got fat the year my father got chickens and I realized why the cows came to Metzger's in the spring and disappeared in the winter. The world was changed, the house, my father.

I was eight years old, standing at the window, squeezing my fists until they ached down into my wrists and arms, hoping the plump hunting men of all ages would fall out of our trees and break all their bones and lie there dying on past dusk, into the night. Dreaming of their fat fingers and the thud they'd make on the earth. Wishing it, like a devil.

That year, for the first time, I imagined how it feels to die. Do hands go numb first? During? Is it like fainting? I terrified myself starting those sensations in my body, with my worry.

Of course, the farm is retired now, with machines rusting in the barnyard. The long narrow chicken houses stand empty, and my father is a ghost. And maybe his ghost is standing in the field along with his father and his old army buddy and the young couple a truck driver hit on the road by mistake, but you could never see them through layers and layers of the ghosts of all the chickens my father sent to death. And you could not see Metzger's place through the cow ghosts on it. It would be so dense a fog. The kind you wouldn't dare drive in. A white night.

My father's farm is a three-hour drive to Chicago. And in the city the glass is fine. Fine things, delicate and light.

THREE

Across the field to the north, next to Tim's, is Metzger's, and we share County Farm Road, electricity, sunlight, moonlight, and the word "cat." Although when Bob Metzger says it, he means to do something terrible, and I mean someone I love.

Metzger's is the most unsympathetic corner as far as you could walk in two days. Towers like steeples, barn like a bad castle. Too dangerous for lightning bugs to blink, for worms to move inside their tunnels. The turkey vultures make cyclone clouds above it during the day. And at night, the moon hangs over it.

But when you look toward Metzger's farm, you don't spend much time thinking about the moon unless you're asking why it agrees to shine here, over the things Bob Metzger does to cows and pigs, over panoramic gunshots surrounding the deer eating—moments from danger, the train rumbling otherworldly heavy and its shrill whistle, the geese warning each other on the invention of guns, re-learning it as a new nature, uglier and meaner than the last. Is this, Moon, what you are lovely over? Is this where you direct your pretty light?

I wish away Metzger's farm like I wish away Tim's place. And all his weapons and his evenings making pop pop sounds at mannequins of deer.

FOUR

After two beers, Mom says that money is how men make slaves of people. Specifically, her, and by extension, me. She says, on all of this flat land, the killing men invent permission out of the quiet that hangs like mist over the fields.

Because they want all this—she waves her arms hostilely over her head—for their work. They want everything flat and empty so that they can drive or walk like cutting through butter. For their work.

My mother says all men come from women and all money comes from men.

Money is the thing that says to the working men and the farmers that I have a right to live in a house next to a willow tree. I hold it in my hands. Coins, heads. It does not feel like it belongs to me. It feels like it came from another place or another time. Nowhere near here. From no one like me.

My mother says money is how men make slaves of people. Has us scrambling for our survivals. Desperate. She says they're laughing at the very trees standing in the ground. And that laugh is everything we know about the world now. It is the life we live. And that's why we both work at the grocery store all day under the fluorescent lights, missing the sun.

I was born deep in the hole, debt like barbells, weight plates. My mother gave birth to me and immediately started trying to dig me out of it. And when my father was still alive, my mother and I would work ourselves up internally to extra-value the things he did so that we could act appropriately grateful, like keeping the gods calm and pleased. It became a familiar ritual—learned like cleaning carpet stains, toilet bowls, things that, by the time a girl is twelve, thirteen, she just knows how to do. My mother says, you know how women pretty much view work: pleasing men and making money are pretty much the same thing.

At three beers, she says we are the pets of working men. And when we become unpleasant, we jeopardize our survivals. She says that living with a killing man is all about expectations. You support the accumulation of money. And decide to look at the little sweet things you've got. Like air. And light. And temperature. Bags of food and those four walls. My mother says, money to make slaves of people. But, in our case, this far away from a big city, the local men don't have enough money for that, so they use guns.

I believe her. I have always believed her. She knows when the cats are thirsty sometimes even before they do. She is my only connection to the invisible parts of life. The parts that will swallow me when I die. So I do not dream of my wedding or of some city money career. If L and the cats have no place there, neither do I. I want to live where the deer and the rabbits live.

The grocery store is more than enough civilization for me. Too much when you know what my mother and I know about the killing floors that underlie it. There are three slaughter-houses within five miles of here. The cows lie in the field next to each other. And then their bodies are ripped apart and wrapped in plastic, displayed in the store full of people in their clothes tapping around like cheerful vampires.

FIVE

It is the wettest summer in recorded history. The cornstalks have grown past twelve feet tall, and old men are having their wives take pictures of them standing next to the fields.

On their days off, if the weather is good enough, the farmers and factory men—all hunters, and so all killing men—hoist themselves up on top of brick walls or settle into lawn chairs along Claypool's little Main Street and extend their necks like turtle heads. And with an exaggerated casual, they lick their lips when they don't need licking, or yawn when one wasn't really coming, and settle heavier into their seats. They watch the road for rebels and defectors. Approval fits like a glove. The law fits like a glove. Nothing lost. Nothing sacrificed or given. That warm feeling, warm soup poured down the throat. Full security. The right side of wrong

They say that freedom isn't free because all of the killing men hold a piece of it like shares in a company, and so we had better care a lot about how they get along. In Claypool, they started two motorcycle gangs. Harleys and Gold Wings. They cruise down the streets of Claypool on weeknights and weekends. Late at night, they shoot their rifles up into the air.

SIX

The warm summer weeks wrap around me like thick ribbon. Walking alone in the evenings, silent means still and vice versa. In the fields, the hay rounds are taller than me. Heavy hills, little mountains, like giants with voices so low you can't hear, like big, loose rubber bands. Standing in the languageless grass, I can almost hear the hum of luck. And in the field, the space makes me feel like I could be at the beginning. Of everything. Like there could be a beginning. And that my father's world, the killing men's world, could be a story.

This is a place where alive things become men's things. Money and words. I see them made out of thin air. Out of a body. Seeds and eggs.

On the way to work, I pass the four horses in Tim's field across County Farm Road, and we look at each other. How did I get here, and you get there?

I get peeks at the day. Slivers of light through windows. Moments of weather walking from building door, to car, to building door. My life is not really mine. It is dependent on how men decide to dig. And on whether they have their wars. What they burn and send into the air. What they touch and how they move.

And the process of men making things theirs congeals in the heat or in the cold, into a speed, a train of thought, a momentum.

Still, the white moon in the black air. And the rabbits who hide from me and know a million things about the world that I do not. Air and temperature, sleep and water.

SEVEN

Another hot, humid, summer night. I fall asleep. I dream that we have centaurs in our field. They just appeared one day and will not leave. We have a centaur problem. They are eating everything. I am stuck on the farm with them and they throw women across their backs like they were picking cattails.

Centaurs in our field. At night, no longer just the chirps of frogs in the marsh, but their chatting. Those men's heads chatting later and later into the night. Quarreling, strategizing. And eating all of the apples off our trees. I want to say: "I can hear everything you guys are saying! I hear your plans! Keep it down!" In my dream I get closer to them and they turn out to be men on horseback, but I'd rather they were centaurs who used their own long backs.

The sound of men chatting gets louder. I wake up to the sounds of actual men talking in our field, maybe twenty yards from the house. At least three of them. The sun just beginning to rise.

I listen to them talk to each other in low short words. And then I hear a gunshot.

I run into the backyard and yell, "go away!" into the cornfield. I listen. Nothing. "Get off the property!" I say. "No hunting here!" Still nothing. Then a shot. Close. I jump and involuntarily scream, high-pitched. Then I hear laughter and the bodies of men moving slowly through the tall corn.

I go back inside. My mother is standing at the window, looking worried and shaking her head. I lie back down and sleep again, but don't remember if I dreamed anything else. This time I wake up to the sound of Tim's tractor idling near the house.

EIGHT

Tim farms our property. He pays my mother six thousand dollars a year to plant and harvest corn or soybeans, so he believes he can come onto the land whenever he feels like it.

Tim planted corn this year, like last year, even though he is supposed to alternate soybeans every other year for the soil.

There is a spring on the property that, over the years, has formed a small lake in our field. Tim complains about it to my mother and has tried many things to dry it up. No matter how many times he tries, the lake fills itself.

Tim in the backyard on his tractor with the backhoe attached to it. I tell my mother I hate him. When will the outdoors get some relief? The things the killing men do in the fields and in the woods and in the barns, I can't tell you all of them. I pretend they are in movies. All ketchup and camera angles.

Tim has a musical dancing snowman doll in his truck called Hunter Snowman that wears a tiny camo vest and plays "Another One Bites the Dust."

* * *

The deer have always been nomads as far as we can tell, but Tim built a fence they can't jump over. God knows how he figured out the exact minimum height. So now they sit on his acreage, the lee of the hill depending on the wind or toward the sunrise, sunset. Becoming other creatures now. His creatures. Domesticated. Like me. And their survivals now are decisions about hiding or approaching him when food is in his hands. Not trees or weather, but his round head and dangerous moods and dangerous hands. Something taken. And nothing given they didn't already have.

Then, the free deer who start in the mist in our field in the morning and end up dead in his field by afternoon. His field, our field, such silly names for he sits there, and I sit here, not too far off. Just bodies. Sitting and waiting. Heavy and slow-moving. Just bones. I pretend the walls are invisible. That all things men build are secretly transparent. And the odd dance we do from living room to kitchen, around counters and chairs.

Standing in the house, looking out the window, I am idle. Idle as the llama standing in another fence on Tim's field. I fantasize about locking up Tim in one of his homemade outbuildings and rescuing the llama. And I would bring her back to the house with me, and then we could stand at the window together and watch and wait.

The llama, says Tim, will guard the sheep he's planning to buy. I hate the way Tim uses words. He says llama and the llama is already his. He says sheep and the word itself makes it impossible for him to lose. They are his things. Rightful. Like his money. And he'd have the sheriff here so fast.

Every day I am sorry that I do not find a way to save the llama Tim has trapped in the field he inherited from his dead parents. Every day I fail her.

Tim makes things out of animal bones. Last month he finished a chair. Completely out of animal bones. He keeps it in his garage. When I look at Tim, I think of the pile of animal bones he has. He once told me my femur was probably about the same length as a doe's.

Tim is my enemy, but I am polite to him in the grocery store and at Walmart. He waves to me on County Farm Road. And he wants me to marry him.

One night, at the bar where I once watched a man sleep standing up like a horse, Tim said he would love me forever, and I could just lie there and be loved like suntanning.

And then he hugged me and told me I was beautiful, and that he had once shot a dog running toward him in his field. Head the size of a lion, he said.

NINE

On County Farm Road, as they drive by, the neighbor boys roll down their windows to yell at horses who are naked standing behind wire fences in a small cleared field. The geese are like chubby little girls. Mocked and chased. The boys throw things out their windows at them and laugh. It is a meanness that will not recognize itself, that has no reflection, that conveniently recedes just at the moment before seeing.

In high school, I used to find dead raccoons on my windshield, once the teenaged boys found out I wouldn't eat meat or eggs or cheese. Back then, I imagined the boys as baby demons with their milk teeth, biting into soft white things. And all this huge space. And no one to say what is evil, what is mean. If it is inside of you to know, it has probably been bred into a whisper. Some men never had it to begin with. Empty as the center of an eye.

My mother still cries out when we pass trash bags and boxes in the road. Stops the car. Runs up and hopes there are not kittens in there. Thrown away. To be hit. Once you see one, you will always check. Here, in the place where animals become ghosts. The exact point.

I don't know how life really is. If it's hard and dark or soft and easy. All my life is mitigated by objects men made. Men who believe a thing is for taking. Men who whip horses, who think up the ideas for miles per hour, clearcutting, and making animals sick on purpose. I don't live in life. I live in a world they have constructed. How could I trust it?

My mother says that nature is indifferent like the cashier at Walmart. Taking precious ones and cruel ones, willy nilly and random-like. And maybe she is right, but I still believe there exists that black line, like that is drawn forever between a mother and a child—the black line that connects you to your rightful death, unmitigated by the infrastructure built by human people. Chance and fate and hot air, cold air, stolen from the fawn lying on the side of the road, stolen from her mother, from the possum, the raccoon, so that I, a human person, can glide sixty miles an hour past fields full of broken black lines. It is too easy. I dream of flying like a child dreams of candy.

My life is a floating thing I inhabit. Made strange and dilute, but immune to measles and temperature, aphids and molds.

My father used to say the birds only sing for war or sex. In his world, I am a silly, tiny fish, a minnow. In his world, a man and a horse. A man is simply the less kind thing, and saying it calmly makes it true.

Men breaking horses like rain floods a field. It is like vertigo to let the thought come that it could just be their made-up idea and we're following along a set of terrible neighbor boys so that they don't set our hair on fire on the playground again.

I suppose it's all too big now and late now anyway. The fields are filled with trouble. Same fields that, as a child, I breathed in like a sweet smell, pretty as a fairy tale. But now I know they are full of trouble. And when I drive past them, I try to keep myself from looking. Because that is not a vista, that is the men's handiwork. Lousy with guns and orange hats between corn rows.

I don't know why death and suffering have to exist. But, I do know that nothing has ever existed as cruel as a killing man's idea. Keeping and caging.

My mother tries to comfort me there is just extra mean-ness fallen on the world like a blanket of snow for no reason, right now. I can see through her hair in the sun when the sun is behind her like a soft, white dandelion, like cottonwood.

TEN

This morning, shots being fired somewhere close, but I see no movement. It continues for more than an hour. It is the killing men. Each shot represents the death of a thin deer or a wild turkey walking cautiously through a square of woods. It could make you go crazy if you let your mind stay on it for very long.

I stand in the yard, looking out into the field. Could I stop them? Are they in our field? Are they close? It is maddeningly vague, like not being able to get a straight answer.

It is not enough to have money to fence in the farm. Although men speak to each other in fences, they cut my mother's in order to climb up Corduroy, a three hundred-year-old oak tree, and nail deer stands from Walmart into him.

Threatening to call the sheriff doesn't work—they are each other's uncles and nephews and hunting buddies. Yelling has no effect. Just another woman's nag. You need the actual man there. His truck, his tractor, him cutting the grass as the neighbor boys pass the house coming back from work. And then maybe they'll assume he has his own deer stands nailed to the trees and stay away.

I walk the perimeter of the farm in the evening, looking for signs of the killing men. It is all I know to do. Yesterday I tore down another deer stand in our woods and, walking home dragging the long two-by-fours behind me, I mistook a tall deer for my mother coming out to find me. Our eyes met, and then she dove into the tall weeds, her back legs high into the air. Me, moving through the field in my slow, heavy way, and she, moving through the same field. For a moment, our world. No killing men on this little part of the land, just us. And I would not hurt her, and she would not hurt me, like a wish come true.

*　*　*

I drag the pieces of the deer stand to the house and leave them in the basement. Then I walk toward the cattails and the sound of bullfrogs. The geese, frogs, ducks, and herons have made a community at the little lake that the natural spring made, that Tim is always after. It is our secret lake. Most of the land in this part of Indiana wants to be wetland, but the men go through all of the fields and put in tiles to dry them out. Somehow our lake formed anyway, like a gesture of mercy. Tim sees it as resistance.

The lake brings all kinds of wild things to our field, including one very large muskrat, much larger than average, and when I first saw her, I thought she was a thirty-pound dog. I felt like I had seen something no human had been lucky enough to ever see before. God knows if Tim saw her, he'd want to catch her and show her like a trophy.

I leave a few small, early apples from one of our old trees on the bank of the lake and sit on the opposite bank and watch. Once in a while, the muskrat appears, and I watch her crawl out of the water and take an apple in her hand and eat. Her tail is at least three feet long and hangs over the bank into the water. I told my mother about it, and she told me it was wonderful and not to tell anyone else. So that the men would never find her.

ELEVEN

My mother taught me to lie. Beautiful, round, smooth, perfect lies.

They say you can't please all the people all the time, but I secretly decided I would be the first. And my mother was so proud of her polite little girl who could bend along the arc of the membrane that separates the preferences of people.

She taught me to be a pickpocket, a manipulator of the smile, the embrace. Artful.

She said when she gets around the men, she feels like a fifty-year-old cheerleader. And I picture her in the home-made Minnie Mouse Halloween costume she wore one year and the way my father laughed too hard and for too long.

My mother taught me to be quieter around people if you want them to like you, and also more agreeable and positive about life and everything that happens. This was based on a series of experiments she performed starting in third grade Claypool Elementary School—because she said she always got too loud and when she was angry had the tendency to get over excited and call people Nazis, which made the farm kids squirm.

In middle school, she deduced that being thin made a girl more widely liked, so she didn't eat for ten days. Ten days of no eating. She told no one. That man in India put him-self in a cage in the middle of town, charged money, but my mother did it in her upstairs bedroom, staring out over the cornfields hollow as a drum—Claypool laid out below her like a kingdom made up of all the people in the world.

It is just like her not to know what she had done in terms of money or how men make status and time and the news. Up in her room, holding her belly, quietly watching the men talking and smoking cigarettes on her father's gravel driveway below.

TWELVE

Claypool is invisibly civilized. Not many buildings, but the order, the money, and the pace. Tractors and semi-trucks, corn and soybeans standing in perfect lines all summer, like measures of time. I can see them from two fields over, hear them over the sound of the big snapping turtle breathing, L breathing, all the birds and then the frogs at night. The world nobody has a use for. And I am with them.

I live in my father's house with red brick and white trim, but there are tiny moments when I close my eyes and I do not live in the world of men anymore. Instead there are crickets and geese and cold wind and warm wind. The willow tree.

But then in the evenings, across the field, I can hear neighbor men talk between deer stands. Abdomens like beach balls. And I feel primitive in my ache for safety and warmth for L.

I love L, and L does not live in the world of people. He lived on his own in the woods and now with my mother and Mary and me in my father's house.

My mother says, if there is one idea that underlies the behaviors of people, it is that human beings are the absolute priority on the planet. And if you could love someone not human, everything would be short-circuited and fall apart. L is not a human and loving him makes success look silly and mean. A game for humans only.

My mother says that the outside is real life and the inside is just a building, a big box, not a journey to success, not a journey to anything.

THIRTEEN

My mother and I keep our silverware in Rubbermaid containers because, for most of the year, a dozen or so mice run in and
out of the house, and we got tired of having to rewash spoons
and forks in the mornings after they'd had their nights in the
drawers, and we'd find their droppings like dark grains of rice.

Last spring, in my bedroom, I watched a mother mouse
teach one of her babies how to scavenge for food. The baby
was shy and didn't want to run toward the light I had on.
The mother kept returning and urging the baby to follow her.
The baby would get a foot out of the shadow and freeze for a
moment before running back. Finally, the mother compro-
mised and convinced the baby to follow her under my desk,
a bit shadier, safer feeling, I guess.

I watched the mouse learning to survive for twenty
minutes and a man knocked on the door, and I was pulled
back into the world of trucks and money. His propane de-
livery truck running in the gravel bringing back the order
of things. I handed him a check. I said something small, a
little something.

He left and it became still, but the house was itself again,
a man's thing, and the mice were gone.

FOURTEEN

It is Saturday. The men came early, a caravan of trucks. Woke us at seven, the sound of engines, brittle gravel. They're putting in tiles. Without our permission.

Tim wants to dry up our secret lake to have an extra five acres to farm. He is determined to bury enough drainage tiles to be able to plant it next year. At least five men come to dig.

I am overcome with worry for the big muskrat. Not just that they would drain her lake, but see her, catch her, hold her up like the men in photos holding huge dead fish. Records for the weights of their bodies.

Tim hauls in a twenty-foot-tall thin metal tower. The pounder. Cutting deep grooves yards down into the ground near the lake.

I hear the first crack at the soil like a metal bat landing on a body. There is resistance where the men meet the land. You can see the casualties. Some of them run away like deer. Disappear. Some of them don't have time to run and so they are cut in half or flattened. It is not beautiful like growth, like how they say about building or construction or civilization, how they paint it in the news or in school or on the television. The open soil smells like blood and is dense with working, eating, sleeping creatures, too many to count. And this is the day they are invaded, doused in heat and pressure.

Once, some men got together and built a road, and it was just rock. But now the word for it is "official" and the word for it is "day," and the rest of all else—us, the animals, the ground—is called "the periphery." Extra things, things in the way of important, official, real things like the road.

Raccoons, their bodies for miles on the sides of the road. So that boys with their shirts off can drive their two-ton trucks.

* * *

I don't know where the men get their things. Posts and metal pieces. Tim goes to town and they whisper it to him. How it all fits together. Like a secret history. The origins of town, its genesis. How to maintain it, extend it. The revelation of order by men. Tim has received it and now he walks so confidently.

I walk fast to the lake. Tim is not there, but Gary. Gary tells me Tim forgot something in his garage. So, I wait. "Where is your mother?" he asks. And I tell him she's not home even though she is.

Gary works for an excavator. He crosses his arms and says it looks like rain and that acid rain is a hoax, you know, that god made rain acid on purpose so it would sink down into the ground better. And he says that all weather is due to solar flares and that's what the people don't tell you when they talk about global warming. That's the reason people still can't predict the weather, because weather has nothing to do with pressure and clouds, but with sun flares god made and decided on. So all

     THE PLACE WHERE BUILDINGS GO

weathermen are full of shit. Pardon his French, he says.

I stand in the field while an agent of death, a killing man, a killer of coyotes, of deer, of almost anything on the planet, explains to me the nature of the universe.

He is absolutely sure. Certain. He has passed enough years and watched enough television, heard enough anecdotes, and that feeling of being sure must have grown. He says without saying: Why not me? Why not me know something? Why not me sure when things seem it? He thinks, just because he digs holes for a living doesn't mean he can't be certain in his knowledge of solar flares. I imagine him in a situation room at NASA, his sweaty gray t-shirt in the icy air conditioning.

Gary talks about Indiana. Talks smoke out of his mouth. He doesn't know anything I don't know. We both grew up here. My mind is his mind. What is it that makes him feel so certain? What is it that makes him a killing man and me a woman who'd be prouder to be a deer?

Tim pulls onto the field. Happy to see me. Yells hello too loud. Walks over to Gary and me enthusiastically. I start by smiling. Then I say, "Tim, we want the lake to stay."

Gary, and three twenty-year-old boys who Tim hired, and Tim, look at me.

"Really." I say. "We'd like the lake to be left untouched. We really need you to stop." I say.

Tim opens his eyes wide and just looks at me for a few seconds, and then he says well, he's already gone to all of this trouble and he's paying for it and so they're going to need to go ahead. And I tell him I'm sorry, but it's not his land. He says that I might owe him money if they stop. Money for getting it all together and for what they've already done. I tell him I don't owe him money. He tells me I might again. And he looks at me for a long time. I don't say anything. And then I just say, "Please, Tim." And then I put my hand on his arm.

Tim looks at my hand and then at Gary, and Gary shakes his head. Gary says, "This ain't right." Gary says, "C'mon Tim," but Tim believes one day I will break down and marry him, so he pauses. Gary repeats, "This ain't right."

I don't know how long we stand like that. Tim shrugs his shoulders and says to pack it up boys. Gary is angry. "It's your money," he says to Tim, and slams the bed of his truck closed so hard the tires bounce.

* * *

I look down at the deep groove full of mud. A line halfway to the muskrat's lake. And I stand next to it while the men load their things and finally drive across the field in their line of big trucks that bounce hard as they pull onto County Farm Road, and then make their engines loud as they glide away.

Then it is just me, for a while, alone with the deep groove with water sitting at the bottom. I've made myself conspicuous. My getting in their way, red like a light. Drawing fate's attention and Gary's attention. Drawing in the anger of men.

What is the opposite of a building? The sky? A thought? Sleep? Worry.

I look at the lake. If the muskrat were small enough for me to carry under my shirt maybe I could protect her, hide her.

If I could, I would drink the lake, carry it in my stomach through a desert to Russia or Alaska. Wait until dark, check right and check left and then spit it out. Swallow and relocate everything else, all the outdoors. Leave the cities alone in space, surrounded by a perfectly still cold. Isolated and clearly defined. Far from soft or warm things, like the barn cats having their babies or L playing in the rain, the humid heat of the baby birds and mice growing up in their sleeps in the false ceiling of our house, behind the laundry room walls.

But I can't. And the men are always coming. Like a train.

FIFTEEN

Since I was a little girl, I've worried about what I was going to do when I got old enough to have to have a job and money. To leave the cats' days and the time outside. To be surrounded by people in a room, with their ways of ordering things, and their jokes, and their insistences that they are more important than cats and deer and insects. That they can have their ways with them and kill them if they feel like it, and then just have fun.

I grew up watching the deer and wishing they would take me in as one of their own and let me join them. And we would walk through the fields and find places to sleep, and I would learn how to eat just the grass, and we would have each other. And my father's world, the world of people, would become as tiny and far away as a star.

As a girl, I spent most of my summer afternoons lying still as a log in the grass with the sticky-eyed kittens. They crawled over my body like my body was just another hill.

The money world felt like punishment—school, and teachers, and a system of roads that constitute what I guess you could try to call human survival. But, to me, it was still just the killing men, a step removed and dressed in clean shirts. The rabbits and deer and flies are surviving. This is something else.

I was scared of growing up and having to get a job. I wanted to hide from money. To postpone the long stretch of days to follow high school or college during which one has to eventually accept her position in the world of the motions of men. Workadays and designated entertainment spaces. Units of time. Spectator, witness. If not successful, married, if not married, wishing to be married, if not wishing to be married, lying and secretly wishing to be married. To postpone the moment I was no longer a child, a creature, a growing thing among growing things, but now a woman living in the world next to Tim, who happily makes plenty of money for himself by killing, trapping, and selling llamas, sheep, deer.

All of my days stack up next to the killing men's days, like Tim, who just got the polishing position at Zimmer and makes three times the money, and if you get a knee or hip replacement, Tim may have polished it smooth in between killing young mother deer and building a meat smoking room out of reclaimed barn wood.

* * *

My mother and I work at the big grocery store in town. She has been working there since I started grade school.

I did not finish college, and my mother was kind about it because she did not finish college, either. She said you had to have the stomach for it, like Sunday School, and we did not. My mother said she would get me a job at the store and that I would not mind it too much, since she did not.

I am a cashier and my mother is a shift leader, which means she still checks people out on lanes, but she also works the self-check and the customer service desk. They do not let us sit at the cash register. Everyone must stand—no matter who you are or how long you've been there. For the first two months, after my shift, my legs and feet were swollen, and my mother showed me how to prop them up on two pillows in bed and lie there for at least an hour to let the blood come back down. L would lie next to me and I could feel my heartbeat in my legs. I don't know how the other women, who are mostly in their 60s, do it year after year. They do not complain, and they are also not always nice. They are trees made of harder wood than me.

When I am at work, I pretend that I am sitting up in the top corner of the building, against the ceiling, watching myself ring people up. When I say something, I hear myself say it from a distance.

Birds get caught in the building, mousetraps and poison in the break rooms, the lobster tanks. I don't look at them. Because I do not ever want to become used to it.

The people shopping are rude and in a hurry, and the old men call me honey, and I have to pretend that I am happy to be there and to have the job. All day, I miss L and the cats. I think about what they are doing when I'm waiting for an old woman to find her coupons. I picture P and her kittens lying in the shade. The old woman says, "hello in there," and she's been holding out her shopper's card and I say I'm sorry and scan it.

None of it is how it feels. There was another dead young mouse this morning in our front yard. There are tiny insects and worms with no chance against a day's traffic. Then the chickens, the cows, and all of the sounds of good luck and bad luck happening in even the tiniest of ways, both outside and inside. Everything happening all at once. But I have to remember the number for bananas, and the names of things, and the time, and to count backwards the change out loud, and when to offer a penny to make the change round.

At the end of our shifts, I drive my mother and myself home. The fields are black and I drive until I see the single yellow security light my father mounted on a telephone pole that hangs over his house, which is supposed to be our house now, but feels like it is ours about as much as a dollar bill does. Inside, L and the cats will be hungry and there will be Mary listening to the TV.

SIXTEEN

For more than five years, my grandmother, old Mary, has lived with my mother and me. She is bedridden, with fractures down her spine. Mary's bones are becoming coral and becoming lace. Wood and then cork. Age blew holes through them like the mountains in Utah—if her pulse were the wind.

My mother stays up nights hoping Mary's bones will hold as if they are a structure she's built herself, and the time she spends sleeping means leaving something rickety out in the weather, something she should have built better to begin with.

In the morning, in her bed, Mary slurps her soup and belches and finishes her juice just in case her mother, old Josephine, is a ghost behind her. Josephine was a preacher, the first female preacher in northern Indiana. And Mary was taught to accept a room, a man, a physical position, the way you accept weather.

Mary says it was very hard to learn to wait. That's what she called it—waiting. The hardest thing she can remember doing. To learn that a man is a man forever and forever are we in his wake. But, boy, her mother did a good job teaching it, she says.

Mary found, as with all of men's dealings, there were benefits to going along with them. When she had her own house, it was full of mousetraps and small lacey objects. And, even now, she finds delight in thinking up little criticisms. Which of the furnishings are to her taste and which are gauche? Which aspects of the room might imply sin? Which might be good and right? And this is how she spends her days.

In my mind, I picture a dressing room, a mercantile—the open air markets over thousands of years—women finding pleasures in little objects while the horses fall and work, in a man's wartime, peacetime.

Watching Mary, I do not want to imagine the strange squeeze that will take me from myself to a killing man's wife like Mary and my mother. All of the waiting and accepting and pretending mean things aren't really mean. But, it happens to every woman here who doesn't die or isn't mentally disabled, although there were even attempts to pair Marla, who could not get into kindergarten and so stayed home and helped her mother with housework, with one of the big Miller boys.

I feel the pressure to marry in the air even when no one is around. That my life here with my mother and Mary should be temporary. That a man is coming and could arrive here any day and I'd be obligated to at least give it a go. My mother would never make me, but even she did not manage immunity to it.

Meanwhile, Mom is so tired. Mom is Atlas and Mary's body is the world.

My mother says her days are round as a coin. The top arch noon opposite the low belly of night. I tell my mother I want her to be free, and she says I shouldn't have such clear thoughts about things. That's making your life into an idea. And ideas want resolution. Like a noun wants a verb, a chord wants its tonic. And life is caretaking, and caretaking is a trap in which someone you love needs more from you than allows you to thrive.

And she says, "Here you are saying it out loud and writing it down and asking me questions so that I will come out and say. Yes. I am exhausted, and no, I won't leave and well, now that I think about it, no, I don't have a reason to get out of bed."

She tries to think mainly about the day's weather and says that talking about how hard it all is, and how unfair, is just idea talk. And instead I should focus on the days. Unless I've got her a real way out. Otherwise, see the ways in which today could be softer than yesterday. At least the cats aren't sick. And maybe something amazing will happen tomorrow to change everything. She says, "We aren't solid, you know. Our bodies." She saw it on a channel. They were talking about quarks.

She says that if you keep talking about it, you'll end up doing something to get out of it. And you're trying to keep yourself in it, you see, for the person who needs you. So talking about it doesn't help.

She says, "I'll say this: sometimes I feel as if I'm being filled with helium kicking and flailing as I rise up into the atmosphere yelling goddammit down onto all the tiny people, but they cannot hear me because I have become the light and the air. I am the one keeping the light up. It is my air they greedily breathe. All the while, they find things to complain about. Details. My fashion sense or interior decoration or the house is a mess. Another goddammit and. Nothing. They just keep sucking in, and somehow I have become their creature, their thing."

My mother invented Jesus the person. Gave him specificity and preferences and personality. Because Mary only ever loved him. No one else. So my mother invented him and then mimicked his behavior to try and get a piece of that love. Jesus eats whole rounds of angel food cakes at 3 a.m. to buffer the stress of responsibility for Mary's physicality. Jesus is frizzy and went prematurely gray.

*   *   *

Steve, the grocery store manager, rolls his eyes when my mother has to call in sick to help Mary. She says he makes her feel like a liar. To take care of Mary, and especially of the cats, is not a provably serious thing, one of those things that is not provable to men. It is borderline silly. It is this other world happening in another dimension that is as invisible as a daydream, when the real people like Steve are in real places like big tan buildings with hard gray carpeting. And Mary is just alive with her bones.

My mother does not experience life the way men say life is experienced. A day full of unprovable things, and feelings.

She says that she is always trying to prove that her feelings and thoughts are real, but no one had to build proof around the building and the taking. Or the shiny silver coins that pass over her palms at the register like the most mundane kind of magic trick. Give me that and I'll give you this.

She says that, late at night, when she is falling asleep, she imagines herself as a turtle finding a warm rock and resting on it for a little while, surrounded by cold water, the tides of yesses and of men's machines.

SEVENTEEN

I remember, as a child, believing that my father owned the whole world. As far as I could see in all directions, fields of his corn. And god help whosoever might tread through them. Deer, grasshoppers, aphids, rabbits.

He owned everything to the thick, black line of walnut trees that, at dusk, made the sun set three seconds early if you stood in the right place. And so, everything that transpired, right down to the places the bees liked or where the rabbits hid, was his business. He decided whether they were misbehaving and named their habits so, and so characterized their species. Silly rabbits, dumb possums, naughty raccoons.

He owned everything to the black woods. And in the early evenings, after a day of digging or tilling or whatever it was he did on his tractor, my mother made trips from the kitchen to the gravel driveway for my father and his smoking friends. Sky giving orange to purple, and my father talking about the weather and the government. A fine breeze. The sounds of birds calling, what he characterized with certainty, as sex or war. Brushing his hand across the air, annoying as bugs, the births and deaths of all those creatures. But my mother was smooth as a ball bearing, a cool, slick cat. And I was with her.

Sometimes I think the world of men is like a great ocean. And a girl's life is days spent watching the shapes the waves take as they wash upon a perfectly unmoving shore.

My father took his field the way, every spring, water takes low ground. And, almost immediately, minnows appeared in the clear puddles left after the first rain came down upon his tilling. A field full of fish, and then my father who was not one.

He set into that land like hammer to rock. His movements angry, his face calm.

The field just sat like a girl. Still and quiet, like my mother with her tight lips and eyes hard like glass as if to say all had been seen before, nothing unfamiliar.

Is it dead? The field, I mean. Seems everything has every advantage over it, my father, the water. I have to remind myself that it is not his really. Seems overwhelmingly bleak. That my father and his mean cigarette friends and their bad jokes should have such an easy time taking it. Meanwhile, in the house, I am supposed to read about little girls and little boys and mothers and fathers.

My world was built upon the hush of my mother's voice when she'd speak of people or television shows, the nature of life, patterns. Napoleon could have lived a farm over. The Serengeti was a half-shed tree alone against a bare field at sunset. All of it existed here, with us, my mother and me. All the facts I was to learn in school were the words people use to make their plans, giving us all in class our permissions to do mean things to chickens and to deer the rest of our lives. Convincing, persuasive. Repeated permissions.

My father said nature is just like business. Natural selection, survival of the fittest. He made it true by saying it, because that is what he saw everywhere. But I did not. He said I was just silly and didn't want to, that I was a girl pretender.

I can't remember the moment in my childhood that my internal reality and my father's world became interwoven. His world overtook mine. He slowly became right just by sitting and I had to admit to what was written (science) and to what could be seen (buildings).

With him in the room, the couch slowly became something else. Someone made that couch, bought and paid for that couch, and we, my mother and I, were wrongdoers, borderline freeloaders on it.

There was an immediacy to my father's directives and requests. And then, all of my mother's love and silent worry floating around, and my secret wondering what kind of thing I am and how I'm alive to begin with. My days were swirls of light and vague language. Meanwhile, to my father, I'd better look busy. At some point, I realized I spent most of my days feeling like I was trying to ride a bicycle (his). Trying to stay on (not fall).

Of course, my mother already knew this. She was a good bicycle rider. She knew that her days were his in the practical sense. They were his words and his plans. My father used to get mad when it was too hot outside. And my mother would pray for a breeze for him. So that he didn't take all our heads off, I suppose.

My mother chose my father, his house, over the outside, like staying behind a man in a bar fight. And he could say anything to her. She accepted his hand as the hand of fate, of luck. Instead of asking death's permission, she asked his.

It must be done. An agreement with a husband, a sort of sacrifice to meanness, to its spirit, that filled the room up with heat when it was freezing cold outside. Made me lose my stomach a little when my father was around, like falling from a height.

Like Mary would say, man giveth house, food, car, money, and man taketh away. Anything outside of that was all danger, the outdoors, which, to us, is the same as the unknown. Mary imagined it as all hell and writhing like the first generation of abandoned barn cats who grow thin and desperate, who, unless rescued by some miracle, do not survive. That was what could happen to us.

My father stood like a man with an answer. That with enough hardness, meanness, you can almost escape your own mortality.

My mother kept busy keeping our home. The world outside, a mystery. Hot, wet, cold. And every day she became more afraid of discomfort. Anything small. So much so that he could say all of his words to her and she'd stay put. For all his meanness, familiarity was a kind of comfort she was terrified, now, to live without.

What makes a dog stay in a man's home? Fear? Food? Paucity of love in the world? Paucity of justice? My father would say it was because she is weak or dumb. Not like him. Not hard enough to cream a field and bend it, to make a house where creatures are too scared to leave.

* * *

Every summer, shucking corn in the yard, my grandmother and mother would put husks and silk into paper grocery sacks. All afternoon, they'd squeeze together their thighs tight and chafe under their breasts and arms in the summer sun and nod when my father walked over and spoke. As a child, I looked up at their chins nodding like tipping boulders.

My mother was on an allowance my father doled out slowly, reluctantly, with suspicion in his eye. She was taking what was his and doing with it what we women do—make things invisible. He and his friends would stand on the gravel driveway in the evenings growling about government entitlements with a glance toward the house where my mother was inside quiet—folding laundry or washing plates. Invisible and tense.

So arbitrarily was the site for our house chosen. And the men came and put down blocks and couldn't get much square, but put trim over the gaps. And it stood alright. Plots of land each fitted with propane tanks and septic.

And inside, for my mother and me, became the environment of reality, became law and life. Because the alternative was a swimming wind and the beating sun or the unimaginable cold and no one to teach how to live it. My mother and I were tense and checked ourselves for our warmth and comfort the way my mother still checks her pockets over and over for her dollar bills before leaving the house.

To be this domesticated thing, a man's business. And look out over the countryside worrying that I've offended my father and he'll tell me I'm out. I exist like an invention of his. And I wonder, what is my life for? My father left us in a house without a screwdriver and for all our lives we feel like fools. Even now, I am a guest in his house, on the ground, in the weather. A builder's guest. Money dependent.

I think I used to be an animal like P and the raccoons. A wild thing. Something else. Free to hate the men who kill everything on four legs. Self-sufficient, and a runner. But now I practice being grateful for everything and then I get so tired and have to lie down.

I don't know how to live without following them. I feed L and the cats with the trail of meat they leave. We exist in the wake of their killing days, their expeditions, their "adventures," their explorations. A greasy trail, a blood trail.

And how completely rearranged now are the placements of forests, fields, life and death, suffering and mercy. A creature's natural line overwritten by men digging thousands of years ago. As in: that field shouldn't be there. Placed about as rightfully as a lie.

My mother says that this living is about securing help from killing men, from conquerors. But then there was always the world she and I populated with white cotton, with the cats. Hidden in plain sight. Like a secret unbelieving. I keep it deep inside of me.

EIGHTEEN

Men split the world, and my mother and I sometimes slip through the logic of it like through the lacey shadows trees make. And it has resulted in a winding fence and ramps and tunnels twisting around each other, shooting out of every upstairs and downstairs window of the house. We have built an infrastructure so that the half-tame, half-wild farm cats can have an inside in the outside.

From the road it looks like a mess, but there were reasons and considerations for each oddly-shaped (not straight) fence and complicated tunnel system—cats who need to be separated, cats who have trouble climbing, cats who came from the east field and need to be able to have access to it. The mess is the shape of another kind of civilization, a glimpse of another attempt, another beginning. It is nonsense to the men with minds to make rows out of the thick knots of dark green woods. And they let us know it when they see us.

There is a bad cat virus around the county and my mother takes in the cats who get sick, and feeds them with syringes when their tongues become raw and ulcerated. My mother and I want to keep them safe. What is it outside? Men? Jinxes? The invisible ill will that makes a man mean?

Floating in the air like cottonwood, biting flies. My mother says to make death bust into a warm lit place to get them if it really must. She will dissuade it in any way she can.

My mother says that the world is a dangerous place because of the killing men. She says that they have shown us that an unscrupulous willingness to power over, to kill, is all it takes to reign over all the world. All you need are no scruples.

Sometimes at night my mother says she is afraid she will run out of energy and the ill will will take her and the cats like an undertow.

NINETEEN

This past spring, eight more cats suddenly appeared in our yard, thin and sick with the virus. She is convinced Gary dumped them here. She believes Gary did it to make her kindness impractical since she told him he could not hunt on the farm and that he could not park his truck in the field to sit in it and shoot coyotes, even though he told her his shooting of coyotes was a favor to her and to all the people in the county. Gary took it personally because, apparently, it was also his way of asking her on a date. Now we have more cats to look after.

Soon after we took them in, one of them, who we named P, had kittens. We decided to keep them inside and we hadn't yet fenced in a field for them, so they stayed in our house, but P had within her the knowledge of survival. Something Mom and I never had. P had lived in the woods and the fields and navigated the dangerous county roads and the bored, fat young men with deer mannequins and rifles burning holes in their pockets, who will take shots at anything moving. When the kittens were old enough to get around pretty well, P would call them, voice like a tiny trumpet, and tell them to follow her through the kitchen, breezeway, into the garage—trying to teach them the things she knew about how to survive. They became bored and stopped coming to her when she called and, eventually, she gave up. But P still has it and her kittens never will. And neither will my mother and I.

TWENTY

Night, the stillness, the moon, the buzzing of a thousand tiny, intricate insects. The deer, at night, wade through the knee-high soybean fields. I hear them shuffling the leaves when I walk trash bags full of cat litter to the dumpster. I can hear them, but not see them. Just the moon hanging over Metzger's barn a half mile across the field. I can hear owls echoing in a small block of dense woods. Why did the men spare that group of trees? It is full of rocks and water and animals use it for hiding.

I clean the cats' rooms and give them fresh water and gray-brown ground meat from small cans that pop out like jello from a mold. We get a discount on the canned food at the grocery store. We are traitors when we buy it, but we do not know how else to feed them. We are middlemen now. We negotiate for each cat's life within a system of cascading animal killing. They sleep on blankets and carpeted cat towers. And they kill mice by the dozen.

Why don't I take care of the mice? Spend my life protecting them instead of the cats? All I can figure is that they're smaller. Size. A whole life. Size, mobility, proximity, and luck. So arbitrary is the success in the world of humans, are the decisions in a human person's mind.

A bear's death matters more than an eel's because of what? Size? The bear is larger, furrier? That simple? If I were smaller, my body would probably have ended up in Tim's or Gary's mouth by now. Or, I might be one of the thousands of ghosts my father made.

The mayflies get hours. And my death will be the same size as theirs, just bulkier remains. In the meantime, I feel so tired. All I can think to do is cover the cats with the best good I know of—a mother's kind of stewardship.

TWENTY-ONE

In fall, the corn stands itself up on its roots like spider legs. Pops and thumps of Tim and Gary at night practicing machine guns, firing Gary's cannon, like year-round fireworks. And the killing men shooting in the mornings and evenings and all day on the weekends.

How did I become lost like this? Underneath and behind men moving and talking like a veil. Men having trouble communicating with each other, and my mother and me waiting for them to order their words and then their trucks and deliver the things we need to take care of L, the cats, and each other. Food, cat litter, coated chicken wire for the tunnels and fences.

Am I dependent on Tim and Gary? Their big, thick arms? For food? Shelter? That they do not do something to ruin the land or the sky here? Yes. I try not to make them mad. Then, I sit in my chair in the quiet for thirty minutes, coaxing the flush out of my cheeks. This is what survival is for me now, like the deer caught in Tim's field.

Tim isn't surviving. The killing men aren't surviving. They are killing things that move. And watching movies on their televisions about military heroes, then waking up and practicing their kill shots on mannequins before work, after work, on Saturdays and Sundays. This is not surviving, this thick, too-rich thing, what is it?

How do men become unmovable objects? How do their ideas become systems, buildings, facts? Where do they learn to push on the surface of the earth, to make the light from the sun into official days with the sheer movement of their want-ings, wishings, plans? As if they have been presented with a gift of construction or permission. Kings of the silence. Of the mute outside.

How passive is the planet? As passive as ether. As exposed as air. As dissectible as a soft belly. Just waiting for the willingness to be cruel enough to come over one night and tether the horses to the trees and the oxen to each other.

My mother said she was disappointed to find that life was a thing the boys she went to school with would grow up to conquer in camo jackets or in suits from JC Penney's. And the little drops of love humans give to each other would hap-pen on the backs of horses who the men break and sell and buy and use.

She said she wished someone would have told her that, of all things making survival challenging—weather, tempera-ture, lack of foresight—the killing men would end up being the real danger, the real threat. Capable of disturbing the process of passing survival skills to future generations.

They are the real threat to our existences, she says. The killing men, and then a far second, maybe the cold.

TWENTY-TWO

My mother says that domestication removes one's ability to take care of oneself.

My survival is not my own. It is the kind of thing that goes from a great height to suddenly the ground. Precariously balanced on a system of bad deeds the killing men carry out. Like a plate on a stick, a chair on a nose.

They are the things I cannot do myself. Large scale food production, medicine. And the outside is a strange place with no buildings or directions. If you are alone and you are sick, one resolution is actually death.

My mother had the hell scared out of her by Mary, the best domesticator. The house is a fortress against evil, Mary says. The black swim outside, full of all of those damned creatures scraping by. Writhing in the weather. Only in the home is there peace and quiet and calm. The ticking of the clock. The reliable morning radio. All sense lives in there. The men on horseback brought buildings along with the good word. Brought the good news, and it was a house.

But, our little house is so obviously a thawed out rectangle of dirt kept warm in the winter by fans blowing over a little blue fire. And then us, sitting in it waiting for the air to change, for the wind to make its decisions.

It frightens my mother more than the fear of discomfort that there exists discomfort, and that every girl needs a house built big and strong by her father. What about the cats? And what does that say about existence? The wild rabbits and wild cats thin or not, hurt or not, seem always hungry. And I am still a girl safe in her father's house. With warm iron radiators and thick glass windows. I do not understand the discrepancy, the difference between our existences, but I know it has something to do with what they call the history of civilization and men forcing their heavy bodies onto horses.

When I was a girl, my mother could make a man out of the negative space around her body. Always asking questions and begging pardon. She wanted to leave questions with my father. About safety and death and existence. For him to take care of. And he had no idea. And so, he took action.

My father moved and acted as coldly and uncontrollably as weather, so he became something else. Information. Existential. A source of the same mystery within which all my days are suspended. I have no idea how the fields would look without my father's buildings and rows of soldier-plants. He, making us all right and wrong in ways I sometimes couldn't predict.

I am from a pack of women who worry about not working for money and not giving their husbands enough sex to justify supporting them. Who try to squeeze something out of their husbands. Resolution, metaphor.

That's what we do, I guess. The way my mother would try to turn my father's silence into a love story. His motion, building, pushing, digging—into some sort of sense. Look at what we try to do with the killing in men's hearts. Like worms and earth, turning it over and over with our bodies.

And now, men's days provide structure, a drum beat. A rhythm for the body. Providing movement to bring sleep. I am like one of P's kittens. I wouldn't know how to survive if the men stopped pushing my days around like a wheel, if I were left alone with the outside, with the cold. Men making their kills and wars and militias. Me, following men.

And those brutal explorers brought back the good news that the whole world is at a man's eye level. Laid out like a maze or a crossword. Like a series of tasks. The really big things, mountains, etc.: silly, just. Anomalous.

But everywhere they rode in, creatures were sleeping, soft and numb, humid and warm, and their "explorations" woke them like a fire. Like my mother says, "No noble thing, that, overturning rocks."

Old Mary says that the men on horseback carried news and this was the news they carried. Stories about how they went out and found language and rode it like a race car around the world. Stories of war and of honor or dishonor. This was the point of creation, of genesis, according to Mary.

So agreeable are the things within the reach of a man. Even the rocks will compromise all the way into circuit boards, sands, powders. The men are full of all of that damned will. Those damned ideas.

And in their world, kindness isn't real. It's what women do, like a rest in music. A space. Kindness is a plant that is eaten by less kind things who are eaten by less kind things still.

When it is kindness versus architecture, architecture always wins. It's so much bigger and taller, and it never sleeps. And you can get your picture taken by it.

But what about smallness? Not me or even the cats, but a potato bug, a life lived navigating light and dirt. A crumb of dirt half the size of your body, so then what do buildings matter? A potato bug is just as true as the killing men. They are two equally real facets of this place the killing men think they rule.

The complexity of life, the impossibly light-weight sky. Still the killing men do not know they are in over their heads.

Maybe it's true we're all descendants of the species of human that killed off all the nicer varieties. If kindness is a plant, my father definitely ate it. And the killing men create a momentum with their working. And to it we say: might as well. Like we're sails waiting for wind. Rooms waiting for light.

In Claypool, the women talk callously about mice and huddle toward their men and hoist their fleshly bare legs up and scream. Their thick hair and bitter skin. Humid. All heavy upon their seats. That tiny mouse running for its life. And the women laugh and glitter and adjust their bodies in their dresses and go on thinking of things the killing men might like to hear them say. They still want the men with blood on their hands to kiss them in moonlight.

The killing men have their systems and their wives who try to support them and be agreeable, and I think that maybe the men misinterpret that as permission. As if the sunlight were a smile, the moon an "ummm hmmm," a "do your worst tomorrow again." Sleep: a pat. Done good today. So, here is another.

And we talk nice, we women. Give them the words. We speak of lovely little things. Tiny things. Basil, chives, men's business numbers. All the time I'm remembering how my father hung the chickens by their feet upside down and silently, in my mind, I hold him down and encourage the chickens to peck out his eyeballs. He would have been so angry. And he would have called it a loyalty problem. But in real life, I did not do anything. I hid.

Late at night, the early hours of morning. I would glimpse myself in the bathroom mirror and hear: those eyes cannot be trusted. Those are a swindler's eyes.

TWENTY-THREE

Tonight, Tim comes to the door with Gary. They want the deer stands back that I've been tearing out of our trees. Gary says he will call the deputy sheriff who is also his nephew. I lie like my mother taught me and tell him I don't have them, that I didn't do it, and Gary doesn't believe me and walks back to Tim's truck and slams the passenger door closed. Tim hangs back and says that Gary is not too happy with my mother since she wouldn't let him park on her property to shoot coyotes (kye-oats), and he's not too happy with me since I got in the way of drying out the little lake on those five acres.

Gary is staring at me from Tim's truck. And I feel his anger suspended in that moment, with the pretty sunset behind him. Sitting there with his certainty and his anger, while the birds wave by and a million tiny creatures churn the soil under my feet, and the pink-orange sky, and the sweet breeze, Gary seems odd. Like thunder in snow.

Tim says he is choosing to believe me and walks back to his truck. I go inside and my mother, who had been watching from the door, says that she is proud of me for tearing them down, but that I have to be careful.

Just after my mother closes the door, there is suddenly a single hard knock on it, and my stomach flips over seeing Gary's face in the window. I open it only a little. Tim is waiting in the truck. Apparently, they decided not to leave yet. Gary looks down hard at me and says in a low voice, almost a whisper, "Don't ever do it again. Do you understand me?" I look at him and nod. It is like staring into my father's face.

Have you ever made a killing man angry? It's like courting fire, lightning. They make a malicious weather. I have to remind myself that the angry man has not become an actual tornado, that they are wont to this behavior every so often, the way a cat goes from walking to running, a hiss or a scream. It is language. Bodily. And if he makes death with it, well, it wouldn't be the first time.

And if he tells you he loves you, it's the same idea. Something he might say when circumstances line up. It is no godlier than his yelling. The back of his neck when he won't look at you, the way a cat puffs up if you startle her coming out of the house too fast.

Gary gets back into Tim's truck and they turn onto County Farm Road and drive away. I will not stop tearing down the deer stands, and I know that, eventually, Gary will choose any of civilization's consequences he likes for me: jail, fines, physical violence, or death.

TWENTY-FOUR

Gary has a "No fat chicks" sticker on the back of his hauling trailer and on Mondays after Tim has lunch with him, he comes to the farm to help Tim farm our land.

Gary thinks I am a woman propped up into a comfortable life since my father died and we get to keep all of the land. And that my mother and I trying to protect the deer and coyotes from men like him is uglier than luxury. Compassion and restraint like a fat stomach. Gary sees it as resistance to creating order, and to the men's productivity.

He acts as if there were a limit to the amount of good or careful that can exist in the world, and that my mother and I are helping too many cats, protecting a stretch of land full of too many deer. As if kindness were nonsense, and if too much of it exists, it would fill up the air and we wouldn't be able to breathe.

The dew is on the grass, and the cats are running out onto it. The evening is quiet enough for me to find something in the back of my mind. That Gary is volatile. And, in my world, he is like a fire, squeezing hard and devouring the oxygen like it was his enemy. Full of impatience. He has made himself an authority in his willingness to kill things. He checks on us to put his eyes on us and ask himself internally whether he'll allow us to continue to be free, to live.

After my mother took in the cats, Gary came over and told her it was ridiculous to slow up her life like that for cats, as ridiculous as slowing down your car to dodge moths. After he left, she said she guessed he can think what he wants about the trajectory of a human life—what should touch it, move it, alter it, and what should not. She said that she and Gary are like two parallel lines. Infinite.

Gary lost a finger when he worked at Parkan. They lose about one a year in the big metal cutters, and Gary's number came up. He managed to get on disability and has a lot more time now, to drive County Farm Road, and to shoot at deer and raccoons and squirrels, to put their dead bodies in his meat smoker. He comes into the grocery store in the late mornings when normally it's only retirees and school bus drivers and young mothers holding babies and walking toddlers.

Gary hates my mother and me. He buys big packs of ground beef and big bags of frozen chicken wings and goes through my line even though there are shorter ones and asks me if I'd like to come over for a barbeque and then laughs hard and loud, the kind that sounds like a cough.

My father's goal, on the farm, seemed to be to destroy and then rebuild the outside world to make himself a king or a god. He was on his way to doing it, beating back the weeds and the trees and any animals who walked through on their own power, but he ran out of time. And now, Gary, on his weekends, has all kinds of time. There is no wrong for the killing men. With their willingness to kill, they invent truth. And money. And war.

     THE PLACE WHERE BUILDINGS GO

TWENTY-FIVE

The cows in the field across the road are having their last few days alive, and I am filled with witness like water fills a can, and maybe by next spring, enough witness will have evaporated so that I may contain more.

The mist settles so thick in the mornings, you can't see past the edge of the yard. Reclaimed property from the men like my father. I wonder did the mist have his permission, or to get so hot or not to rain?

Even the cows, I wonder what it feels like to be reclaimed by the mist. I am always lit, surrounded by light, by my mother, and the indoors.

The night is raining in rounds like girls' songs. What is it to disappear? Like the rabbits, the field mice, glimpsed once and simply never heard from again. To be loosed from all men's conversations. Invisible. Lost and forgotten by all of human talk.

I dreamt I was a wild thing, running.

I dreamt I was a wild thing. A poor, running, nothing.

TWENTY-SIX

A young pregnant calico cat with a voice like a thin flute caught eye contact with my mother last week and held it, and my mother added her to her list and left plates of food in the spot where she was standing during that first eye contact, and the cat comes several times a day now, and eats and eats and her ribs move as she breathes and eats.

My mother says that she has dreams of solid things. Like buildings and money. Things that can protect a creature from the killing men, from the roads. What is caretaking's building? Where is its concrete proof? It is easy to doubt yourself at night when you are invisible. The material world slices through a person. Words, kindness, help, conversations about what men's world really is, evaporate like mist while the tractor supply store building stands stable as a mountain.

My mother says we are domesticated things, like the llama. And we bear our discomforts—too cold, too hot, tired, scared, thirsty—in a preternatural state of alone.

I think when I die, I will dissolve like sugar into water, like how kindness dissolves into the air, like my mother's caretaking, like these words. Into a great invisible lake.

TWENTY-SEVEN

There are things you cannot learn from men or books. Things that can only be learned from caretakers. Secrets. The way, in winter, the dead Queen Anne's lace holds tiny cups of snow like cotton bolls. The way the milkweed pods look like perched finches—are they decoys, or just match mates? There are things that can only be learned by not believing the things the killing men explain.

The mother deer who likes to eat in our barnyard had twins this year. Two. And my mother glances over their thick-looking, spotted coats and nods her head. That deer, she says, is a good mother.

When I worry about Mary lying there, nothing to do but wait for her death to come and get her, I lie in my bed and pretend that I am her, and picture exactly her room and her window, the things she looks at. I lie in the quiet and pretend I won't be able to leave my own bed and it is just the soft flow of air through my nose. In and out. And the light. And the dirt and dust, and the tiny gap where wall meets carpet. Thank god for the television.

Putting food in, food coming out, not moving. What does it mean? She is waiting to die. It is unbearable, I say.

But my mother says, no, she is waiting for her lunch, then maybe for someone to visit or to call. For the light to change.

And for a moment, I notice that in between that eating and eliminating, is this glittering thing. Alive. Mary, even in that bed, maintains an impossible suspension. Like the moon hanging in the sky. And that has to be it. Now, that's enough. Enough of an invention, enough success.

TWENTY-EIGHT

In the beginning, there was a vacuum of space. This is Jay. He will explain it.

Jay's father is the president of the bank. We went to school together and his parents sent him to college even though he knew he was going to move back here to work at the bank, which he did. Now, Jay's father is putting pressure on him to find someone to marry, so Jay has begun to call me every couple of weeks to take me out somewhere. He has called today because he has a long weekend from work and wants to take me on a drive.

In the beginning, there was a vacuum of space, and now there are a hundred brown birds sitting along half-frozen water accumulated in a field next to the highway.

In his car, Jay tells me his ideas. He tells me what my blood is made up of, and how the planets move and why they exist, and that my ideas about kindness are simply evolution-arily beneficial.

He says that someday the sky will be completely dark. Empty of all stars. And that right now the universe is speed-ing up. And quarks and speed of light and magnetic fields.

And he is a thin, sweaty man. Pale as ivory paper. He wears leather shoes and ill-fitting jackets. His head reminds me of a blown glass container. Hard, permanent ridges and shaped like an upside-down jug.

And I feel heavy. Heavy enough to sink down through his passenger seat into the road and finally through that into the middle of everything. I sit with my hands together. And he drives me away from the edge of the lovely water.

Jay says that there exists a list of all things men have ever seen and the number of neurons next to them, like the earth were on a journey to squeeze out neurons. More. More of them. Not trees or salamanders, those are just trial and error, décor.

He says that all of my love or friendliness is just a cluster of neurons, and see that cat purring at the edge of sleep? Feels 39% less than you do. It is impossible for that cat to feel more than that, based on neuron numbers. The frogs and flies? Don't even ask. They're practically nothing—really close to being thin air because not only the neurons thing, but they are also small, and there are small things and big things and things sized in between and small things should be bigger but not too big—just right, human sized.

I guess having the perfect number of neurons causes teenaged farm boys to drive two-ton trucks with their shirts off, hitting turtles on purpose and holding the outside of the cab through the rolled down window with their forearms as if it were the side of their own bodies.

And this, after all, must be the goal of the universe.

And the turtles are just too dumb to get more neurons, so they are stuck being turtles like the mentally disabled boy in high school who has to wear a sports helmet all day.

There are no questions to ask. This all started with the big bang. And brought us all the way to Monday night football and we are absolutely on track. Jay promises it is all mathematically sound.

Life is a collection of particles discovered by men who report they are as cold and unbending as coins. An economy of atoms. A government of men.

My father was a chicken farmer, but Jay says I am an invention of modern technology, that my worry and my concern for species outside humankind is the product of luxury time. Conscience.

That it really isn't that I feel compassion for chickens, that isn't the way to think about it, like how I think about the earth and outer space incorrectly, it is more that my system, glands, etc. are overproducing some chemicals which are causing me to have sensations and behaviors. He shows me things on a microscope photo on his phone.

So I don't have empathy for chickens—it is just that my glands are acting up and if you had taken my blood at the moment of concern, you could prove the overabundance, when compared to calm, well-adjusted people. Provable.

Jay says, what I am really feeling are the comforts of modern society. And I should be aware that my concern, for

chickens or cows or anything not human, is basically just another foolish hobby while working men, via money and buildings, hold up the horrible outdoors for me. Over my head like
pillars. Keeping me from being crushed out of survival. Like
the five tree trunks in the basement that hold up our farmhouse. I picture tall concrete Greek figural columns grimacing
down over our field, with the faces of Tim and Gary, their
brows furrowed. Always staring at me. Threatening and ugly.

As if everyone's survival requires killing all the other species and men like my father have volunteered to do it, and now
we are dependent on them like we are on air and temperature
and weather like soldiers holding war off our heads and backs.
Who is a girl to argue about this? Governments and men
doing things far away as the moon.

Jay says this is what it takes to survive, and I should feel
lucky not to be starving and bloated or freezing to death in
the snow. Look at the pictures of children and women from
other countries who are not properly coming into money and
a rational order, who are starving and bloated and/or freezing
in the snow.

The world does not provide food, men do, in the order of
things, and their companies bring money and food and medicine like the sunrise. An actual rainbow is not as much a
rainbow as international trade is a rainbow.

But they don't really know. They don't really know what
it takes. The rabbits do, P does, but they do not.

I listen to Jay turn my life into an idea as if the idea were
its rightful form. The way Jay talks, my days don't become

memories, they become facts, already discovered elements. The equivalents of plain gray pebbles you can always find. Don't worry if you lose one.

I watch as men build the day before me. I watch it like a play. That is supposed to be me. I am that one. I will try to be better at it.

But the days are not ideas. The sky is not an idea. Much to the dismay of my father when weather fell from it.

TWENTY-NINE

Jay's family has paid to bring me to Florida with them to stay in the big condominium they own. My mother says that I should go, and she says that I should not go.

Jay comes into our house with shoes so slick they look like they dripped from space. His shirt is woven with threads that hit the light. He glides through my father's farmhouse with some sort of sophistication, refinement, like a clean hotel room, new computer, flat screen television.

Meanwhile all around us, at Metzger's, at Tim's, is pure crass killing. Dirt and concrete. Electricians' tape. Blood and muscle.

*   *   *

It is either this or lie in bed. I convince myself that the movement of traveling with Jay is saving me, renewing me. A gift of momentum I would be a fool not to cling to, rescuing me from the inertia of the lonely, the rural. Keeping me from becoming my mother, my grandmother. From feeling, so acutely, the darkness of the world.

Jay's family's boat slices through the water like soft butter. Like it was always one day meant to. And I am afraid not to feel grateful. And, on it, I find myself thanking him for the ticket and for the trip.

His earning potential—I imagine tying my fate with his parents' money. He would be able to provide something foreign and mysteriously acquired. When I try to acquire it myself by working at the grocery store, it just comes in drips.

Jay is charmed by the fact that I have not done what rich people do. Have taken no trips, looked out upon no important vistas. He loves that I pack only one bag, small enough to carry onto the plane so that we do not have to hassle with the baggage carousel.

Meanwhile, what am I doing? Sitting in expensive restaurants. Smiling politely while his father and uncle talk about fishing sheepshead. Being taken for a boat ride in the evening off an island during red tide. Hundreds of floating dead fish. His family bunches their faces as if the bodies were eye sores, wet towels left in the bathroom. And, quietly, I am replacing the word "fish" with "girl" and imagining myself floating belly up, ugly and hair exposed, rotting in the way of men's boats and vistas.

The next morning, Jay takes me to the city science museum to look at tiny skeletons and call them long, ugly names.

At the museum, alive hasn't ever been enough for humans. It was instantly fires and rock piles. And now, the city is all smooth and paved and computer space. It caters only to human people. Manifestations of literature, forums for theater. People. Little metal taxi cabs and a rush that is gas-state convenience and certainty.

In the city, Jay's evolution has finally succeeded. He believes this was its purpose, its resolution, like a G chord after a C chord. New cars and fast commuter trains. The speed of convenience that makes worry or thought or kindness or carefulness feel out of place.

For a long while, maybe years, a girl could pretend that it was not all made by men who make animals sick on purpose, that the exciting, easy, speeding city was not held up by killing men with guns, in fields, in barns, and their big trucks and heavy trains.

My mother says that I am too full of words, but don't mistake my language for allegiance to the city. I have no allegiance to it. The city is a lie. In real life, young men nail cats to tree trunks and hang kittens by their paws. And I am relieved to get back home to L, and to my mother, and to the cats.

THIRTY

Science is for winners. I woke up and Mary was sick, for no reason at all. The day can disintegrate like that, like sand through your fingers. The day is not a measure of men's time and progress, it is all anomalies and luck. The science men's stories and mechanical expectations are an affront to actual death. I bend over backward to keep the men's days straight, but they are not.

My mother called the EMS, and when they came, they looked like they were huddled around Mary trying to put water back into a jug using just their cupped hands. My mother and I sat next to her body while it became empty.

Mary is dead, and I want to hide in between the people. Take the money for a one-way ticket to London and pretend that death and this place don't exist. Run. Do whatever they say.

I want to eat science and drink the city, and lay out my clothes so they stay smooth, and pretend like the days were built in a line for me to drive. Leave the moaning for someone else to deal with.

But there is no escape, and all my life I'll be saving the pregnant cats from the storms and the cruel farmers. And there will be more kittens and sick young mothers and tom cats, swollen and sick and mean and hungry.

And I will not dare to move much in the mornings, so as not to scare the wild ones away as they swallow big mouthfuls of cat food without chewing. And, like my mother, I'll be too cold, but I'll wait to put on my coat that I've left in the other room, so that the floor won't creak under my feet, until I cannot stand it, and then a little beyond. The farmers will be out in a little while and the cats may not have time to safely return and resume eating. This will be the one opportunity to help them, so every morning I will wait, and it will take up to two hours.

My mother insists caretaking like this is all there is. Anything else is men's terrible work. The meaninglessness of the city is the equivalent to a boy-crazy girl like Mandy, my childhood friend, spending hours making a perfect cylinder of her bangs.

My mother says that people can convince themselves that by living in the city they can escape responsibility and death, but out here we have no choice but to cast our lots always into a green world where someone is always sick and dying.

And for just one moment, I want Jay or Tim to love me. I want behind their certainty like a wall. I want to forget about dying and the eyes of everyone. Tim could toss me across his homemade motocross bike and wheel me into the sunset in a cloud of oily engine diesel. Jay could drive me away from plants and mice to a concrete glide.

I look at the horizon and think if only I could get across that line. No more of this dying. I could have transportation, maps, and money. Cross that horizon line easy as crossing a "t." I could have a life lived doing that. Over and over, back and forth. Trade messy and painful for a calm, predictable cause and effect. The cleanliness of logic, of documents and phone calls, appointments and professional etiquette, like tea and fine china.

I could talk myself into a marriage like a spaceship, an airplane. Pretend that romance is up there along with stars and hydrogen. An element. Mean but right, people say, like predator and prey, war and sex. No doubting, just gravity, money, and winners.

I walk to Tim's house. I tell him about Mary. I let him hug me, then I walk back home. Thankfully, he does not try to follow.

THIRTY-ONE

Both Jay and Tim come to Mary's funeral and then to our house for the reception.

Tim was older in school, so he and Jay don't know each other well. Jay is wearing a suit and Tim walks up to him and shakes his hand hard. Jay looks small and nervous next to Tim. I tell Tim that Jay and I were the same year in school, and he tells Jay it was nice of him to come and keeps patting him on the back. Jay looks uncomfortable and Tim looks wounded and spends the rest of the time looking at me from the food table.

The reception doesn't last long because people can only be in the front room since the rest of the rooms are for the cats. My mother and I don't like people being so close to them. We are nervous and tense and when Mrs. Hall's five-year-old grandson opens the kitchen door enough to see three of the cats sitting in a half circle on the floor listening to us, my mother puts all of the lids on the food containers and soon the dozen or so old farmers' wives who knew Mary from church, are out in the front yard saying their goodbyes.

Jay tells me he'll call me in a week or so. He wants me to know he had flowers sent to the church in case they don't give us the tags. He hugs me and it is like hugging a wood panel. He says that he is sorry about my grandmother.

A grandmother dying is a thing that happens, he says, and so he is sorry for my loss.

Tim is the last to leave and says he wants me to walk to his house with him, that he wants to show me something. A surprise.

We cross County Farm Road and I can see that he has another horse in his field. A male, he says. He says he got him for free from a guy from the bar. He says he's a real dancing horse. He wants to show me.

The horse is 31 years old and when Tim puts a saddle on him, he starts lifting his feet as high as he can. He goes through an entire routine. I watch him interpret any movement Tim makes as the signal to go through his routine again, and so he does, more and more heavily. Tired. Over and over while Tim laughs.

I burn inside. I look at Tim and he smiles proudly, and I force a small smile and immediately feel that I have betrayed the dancing horse. Standing there without screaming at Tim, without locking him in his house along with whoever made the horse dance like that all of his life.

Tim sits in trees and shoots down at deer. They are beautiful and gold. Quiet and lithe. I feel such rage at him. And I feel scared of him. And I suck in my stomach and respond when he asks me questions. And I smile politely. I feel the rage of a lion, but I am a pet. A small gray, tame cat. A granddaughter of Mary and her waiting.

Tim says to the horse, "See? Maybe she will come live here and be your new mama." And the horse sees Tim's face, looking like he is waiting for a response, and the horse begins the routine again.

And I feel so sick that I would do anything to make it stop, terribly sick and trapped in it like a jail. And then I feel myself start to consider Tim. Maybe if I stayed there and agreed to marry him, I could protect the dancing horse from him. Take over all the horses' care. They would see me in the mornings instead of him. They would have plenty of food and fresh water and I would be on their side. I would try to protect them. I would play it so carefully. Make Tim think I am on his side, but empty his bullets from his guns at night. I could try to talk him out of hurting things, little by little. He'd roll his eyes and act like I was on him to keep his socks in one place or to keep his clothes off the floor. But, maybe I could keep them safe.

I turn to look at Tim and notice a pile of antlers next to the garage, and then I remember inside the garage, his bone furniture. It is a fantasy that I could ever get him to stop killing the golden deer who stand on the horizon lines all around us. And, eventually, after I had signed the marriage papers, Tim would get confident and stop listening to me and letting me protect the horses, and then I'd just be his companion. Complicit in my presence.

Then, Tim says that he rode the 31-year-old dancing horse, "yeah, this horse still rides alright." But, he says he'd have to apologize to anyone else who rode him, for the old horse's bumpy vertebrae. And, I tell him I have to leave and walk home alone.

THIRTY-TWO

Jay calls in a week just like he said he would, and wants to take me for another drive in his new car. And, while he drives, he talks about the bank and the car and spending weekends with his parents on the lake, and his parents are talking about buying a new boat next summer.

Jay talks about life like it's normal. Like he knows all about it. Like he is a comfortable expert. I listen to him invent certainty over and over as he talks, with words, phrases, and tone.

Jay treats life like it is an overhead light, like it is just a platform atop which other things are done, a surface on which to put answers in the form of words. Ultimate clarity and definition.

Jay would love everything to be comprehendible the way Mary loved an allegory about God. Birth, death, and emotion—all those ineffable things that come around inevitably, are granted, so no reason to wonder over them, or for Jay to factor them into equations.

Jay has never helped a kitten find his mother or watched a turkey vulture sit and open his wings in the sunlight, still he points at a group of birds chasing each other back and forth between trees and tells me that they are challenging each other for dominance.

Jay's equations never mention how loud the geese are in the wind, floating just above, how that makes your stomach feel. Still, he feels the certainty of his favorite science writers, giving each other dominion over animals, writing trinities in the form of chemistry and physics equations. So simple, they're cruel.

* * *

And if I could say something true—not lie—to Jay, I would say that maybe adding things together or splitting things apart, like the articles and documentaries he likes to talk about, is not the way to look at it. Maybe a shiny car is what happens when a man thinks of the world or outer space incorrectly instead of correctly. Cutting things open just makes the question of existence into smaller, more pieces. Maybe we are not on a path to truth or knowledge. That isn't god's word or science, that's a paw paw.

I want to tell Jay that I know it is hard to experience the sensation of not knowing an answer or not fully understanding everything. A kind of uncomfortable quiet, not from sounds or small talk, but that quiet in a human body before a word exists. Which is also before a story. The cold without a coat. The frustratingly vague kiss of sunset, of oxygen.

But, I think the cats would say that human people invent the questions and invent the answers to those questions. Just us. A closed loop. And that it is not self-knowledge; it is the way a deer grows antlers. We are not more awake; we are not understanding something more. These logics are like bat sonar, a dog's intricate experience of smell, the cool skin of a snake. Mysterious and given as the body. They come up and down like water levels, still we feel steady, like we aren't moving.

Jay thinks I am naïve, but I think that the words for things are wrong. Horse, cat, road. Tim, his name is not right—it is more like saying the word "deer" when you feel ill.

They are words—cow, pig, worm—for creatures nobody's spent any real time with, even just watching or near. And then, the things everyone decides about them and then also about the nature of life and the universe based on those words.

Telling the story of Tim acquiring animals and machines, with words like "buy" and "ship," walks over what he did with language, like a trail in the woods. Suddenly it is a system and an option and a thing that people can do. Straight-faced. Not calling him a sicko, but calling him Tim, neighbor, farmer, man. Then a hundred people do it. Then they say that they are simply doing a natural thing since there are a hundred of them. Born like this. So no one could be troubled to behave differently. It is a storyline based on callous sentences that make the cats into bothersome items with wording and tone so casual you could almost mistake it for humming or nodding.

Out here, our language provides a line, like a bar, a tether, so that no matter how terrible a thing Tim's done, or Gary's done—that killing—they can take back hold of it and be carried away from what they did and rejoin everyone else. They can pile tiny words of diminishment on it, like dirt, to cover all that was done. Washed away with the word "game" or "livestock" or "meat." Words in a sentence that must be all right since they make a sentence.

The words let them continue, like their next heartbeat and then the next after that. They are an infrastructure, like the city. And in the city, people write stories allowing everything to be true and exist together on a neutral plane, as if the meanness were wiped off of everything. All the dancing once the people have let go of something, something true, the memories of the origins of objects, of a tether to kindness. They go on with a motivation, a freedom from taking care and worry. No more urgencies felt.

And, stories turn into vague phrases—a penny saved—that make money sound like it has always existed and its proper management, a product of a fundamental, divine wisdom. God and pith.

My mother says that men are not right about this world any more than any other thing surviving under the sky and in the light. Still, they have come to believe that they are more than a body, that if they read the words of certain men, sit and sleep in their buildings like fortresses, keep a hard heart toward any not-human animal, they could transcend the single body life and live two or three or four glittering lives.

THIRTY-THREE

In a human's brain, if you could open it up and look at it, I think you'd find pipes all hooked up to each other. Connections between systems adding everything together, like all of outside was supposed to form a sum that equals something in the center of a human's brain. So that we blow past survival like a weed by the road, and go on into some strange, dark place before death finds us and shakes its head.

All of these "wonderful" connections like the world's most impractical hat. Making circles, loops. Things that go around and around, over and over, solving themselves like language, fire, and moving water.

They say a human's brain is so good at navigating something, they say as good as a fish is at swimming, a bird at flying and landing on branches. But, what is it? Math? Math is self-solving like language. Based on a logic that begins by setting parameters meant to return to itself, to become itself over and over, so that you think you've found epiphany, but you've really only found another of his words.

Still, the brain can't do its thinking about death, can't do its magic, its worst.

As the deer walk, doing their searching, we do ours. There is no brain in the sky. The trees are not men's beards.

Whatever a human's brain likes to do, they are ideas and they can pass like fevers, a flower without pulling it, like my mother lets them pass while she's helping the cats. Tell yourself stories if that feels good, but please don't try to tack them down with cement bolts, or hire Tim and Gary to do it. Let the stories and ideas sit lightly like the rabbit warrens, the deer tracks and muskrat huts.

We want the outdoors to make sense the way the lizards want the desert. Still, in the falls and winters, the cats take the cold and, within it, find space for sleep.

THIRTY-FOUR

With Jay, in his car, we blow way past survival.

Jay wants to talk to me about what I want, and what he wants, and what we could have perhaps together. He says I can do better than working at the grocery store. For example, he could get his father to hire me at the bank. I could work my way up and end up making good money, he says. And then we could talk about whether we would like to get married and have children, his mother wants grandchildren, or whether we would like to try for becoming successful and rich. He's on the fence about it, himself, but if I had a strong preference one way or the other, that would be alright with him.

He keeps the windows up and the air is stale. Claypool looks soft focus because the windows have a slight film on them, like windows do.

I should think about my financial future, he says. I do not save for retirement. My mother pays for extra expenses with money from my father's life insurance payments. I will inherit the land, but nothing else.

Money is a train and I will always be running along like a fool who can't remember where food can be gotten if not from a working man's generous coffers, mercurial heart.

The birds, the deer, the rabbits, the caterpillars. Little clusters of failures. Hugging once in a while for camaraderie. Little formations, little groups. Failures, each of them. Big, small, strange, oddly formed. Maintaining a failure so big and so long, so quiet, that the future world writes nothing of them.

I think about the deer. I don't think they'd mind not being written about. What do they need with men's letters and words?

But, I am not supposed to be thinking about deer, I am a human person, so I am supposed to be thinking about my money plan, and about what I want.

I don't think I remember what it is to want something. In school, my friend Mandy wanted things. Watches and earrings. She cried for days about wanting Calvin Klein jeans. And she wanted a boyfriend. Woo boy, did she want a boyfriend. She'd wake up early before school to make her bangs into a perfect tube and would often burn her own forehead with the curling iron, but the bangs would be there to cover up the marks.

What is it to want something? My mother never said it, but it feels like somebody without saying, said: go off into the world, find some bureaucratic problem to make your own. Go make some small administrative problem, your problem.

I think I am supposed to find a way to create the illusion of forward motion for myself. A narrative like that. A story of success, dreams, loss, and achievement. The string it is my job to carry my stretch of road. Five feet, ten feet. Enough to at least cover inflation. Cage in my feelings and ideas with the sensibilities of the time, and there you have a shape.

There are collections and subcollections of advice, mag-
azine articles about health and success, modern wives' tales
about proper garbage collection and tips for parking your car.
The world of men is laid out logic like a road. And if you don't
follow it, you're a raccoon. A horse.

Building is for winners who say that life is meaningless
as a cow unless you build something concrete. Do something
real. Don't want to be a girl. Don't want to be a cow.

I feel like I am trying to want things like trying to find a
word. To give shape to my life.

In the wanting world, women let out their hair and snort
over their misfortunes atop horses with their own ribs and
hips. Horses who have had to learn to equate moving with
being bridled and ridden.

They say it is something human, in all of us, the impetus
to war and to build nations, and that I will die without it. That,
without it, there is no story, which means I am not real. I am
lost unless I find some way to insert myself into the buildings,
the institutions, the leather chairs, and social interactions. Instead, I spend half an hour watching lady bugs climb up and
down blades of grass while P sleeps near me in the sun.

I wait for the wanting to come like a womanhood. A
modern American rite of passage, so that time takes on a sense
of forward motion. You had better go find something you
want quickly, or you will be lost forever.

What do I want? It does not come. The wind blows over
me like it blows over a rock.

My mother says that success is just a word that dissolves

on a man's tongue, so that he has to ask for another and then another and another.

* * *

Jay brings me home, and we sit in his car in the gravel driveway. I want to get out of Jay's car so badly, back to the air and the night and the space.

I start telling pleasing lies and half-truths like my mother always did to get out of things with my father. I tell Jay that I am holding him back, that I am going to have to stay on the farm with my mother forever because she has the same disease that my grandmother had. I tell him that my mother has already asked me, and I have agreed, and as much as I would like to move with him to Indianapolis and work at the big bank for his father, I am held back by family responsibility. I tell him I am sorry and if only I could.

He is quiet and sighs and says he is disappointed and wishes I would have told him before since he only has some weekends off, and if this wasn't going to go anywhere, he could have been investing time in other people. Yes, I say. I am really sorry. I should have thought of that.

Well, this is too bad, he says. I won't be hearing from him again, he says. I say I understand. Jay drives away and I stand in the driveway for a minute after his taillights disappear. I stand in the wind. I didn't realize how windy it was since Jay wants his windows always up.

The air reminds me of when my father used to let me ride in the bed of his truck. Once, the tarp flipped up and cold wind rushed over me. The speed, into the night, I saw in my mind, tiny pebbles, gravel chips, and had a vision of my father's teeth when he was angry or drunk, laughing too much and too hard. Man-wild. Not outdoors wild. Car-wild, truck-wild.

What is this place? That calls up a man's face in my head. Throws my body through the air like a cannonball.

And what is a single dead body to a head full of ideas? Cannot stop to think of the small stuff. Like the moon. Like life, death. To my father, the moon is so slow. It takes all goddamned day to get around the sky. Big and silly and slow. And slow is ugly to a world of people with cars. You need to get back into the car, or you are going to find yourself in your forties or fifties with no human person who loves you. The moon is up there in the night, all alone like a possum.

Money is fast, but love from a human person is even faster. It is like a blur past my body in low light. It is much too fast for there to be hummingbirds whose bodies move like fish in the air, for there to be hundreds of dragonflies bouncing off the tops of goldenrod. Notice them for even just a few moments and approval and love—they are all gone, passed by already.

And a man is always gliding at seventy miles per hour. And if he ever gets done doing that, he is the speed of light. Multiple, infinite, a million moments of expected tasks.

In the world of men, the white moon in the black air is so slow, it is slower than sleep. So slow, it's a place. It is the place where buildings go.

I go inside. L and my mother are lying next to each other in bed, listening to the wind.

THIRTY-FIVE

On one of our walks, my mother says that a weed is an opinion, and that you can say whatever you want to about weeds and they can't say anything back. That's what my father did with style, she says. Making every quiet thing into a word or a tool. Ice is a bitch. Fire is war.

Words become heavy things, forcefields, invisible walls. No, I cannot, no, there is a word there.

She says that words are men's objects we are fools not to learn, like the way we must learn how to get money and use it to buy food, like the way we are fools not to learn which things make the killing men angry.

My father's words were blunt and clumsy like anvils. They rolled over my body, too wide, not nearly fine enough, like his thick hand. Incapable of handling the fine detail of the experiences of a girl who doesn't want to hurt anything.

I learned to take words and say them like spells that work on the men and make doors open or calm a room, because my mother says that the killing men walk the line between cruel and kind, war and peace, and a handful of words can blow them to one side or the other.

And she says that the lack of notice Tim has, for the cats and for the deer, is just a thing for which he was not given a word—and therefore a place in his head. And that is how a language is passed, and how a language makes a place, and how arbitrarily it overlays all the aspects of all the moments under the sun.

I wish I could provide another story of this place, an alternative to Jay's human evolution story, Tim's predator/prey story, but that's the problem with stories, everything is built on the foundation of the old one. And these words are what connect human beings to each other and to our history, ties us to convention, to an underlying belief in the superiority of the human mind.

It is a story that colors the day. A decision to look at the outdoors as a quarry, supported by a history of men wearing the furs and skins of creatures they do not understand. Soot-covered mannequins at the Natural History Museum around bonfires representing a story of desperation, poor prey waiting—until they learned how to kill. And so, the killing men kill things for them, in their memory, because of a story and some mannequins.

THIRTY-SIX

Something mean happened. A long time ago, the first of the killing men were terribly, terribly mean. There are solid gold figurines from seven thousand years ago of bridled horses hauling men's asses all over godknows where, to do godknows what.

They did a string of bad things. Things a mother would instinctively say no to. Taking things, pushing things, killing things. Big things that had always been there. Since, as far as a person might imagine, the beginning of everything.

And those bad, some unspeakable, deeds made a car, in addition to some basic mechanical maneuvers, and a house. And that's where we each live, and now Tim has his house down the road with a heated garage full of dead things.

There is no talking about good here. Now that the men made the cars, and all of the buildings. In everybody's heads now like words. Try getting them out. I wish I could get them out.

Tim really believes that he is meant to do his work. Look at how most things work much of the time. The buildings stand against god's terrible wind. The cars and airplanes break records of speed.

His proof, in addition to car engines and modern medicine, is that meanness slices through the air so easily. Unimpeded. Easy as a dance. And all of my impractical, invisible concern is like weights. And I am slow like a cow.

My not-building, not-killing, not-believing is invisible, is a field, is open space, is free blood. The fool, the stocked lake, the waiting lake.

Cause and effect gave the building men and the science men and the killing men his blessing and so, let civilization ask its perpetual question as Tim's rifle makes its curses in threes: If we are cruel enough to kill and catch and trap, if we can amass enough meat, dissect deeply enough, then what could we find in that new pulverized place?

If we are willing to be cruel, what riches lie beyond? What could we build with the bones? Could it be wonderful, like flying?

Climb that bone ladder all the way up to heaven and peel it open like an unripe orange.

THIRTY-SEVEN

My father and his friends considered themselves working men, trading the bodies of chickens and cows, their insides. Telling the lie that a man's brain is so right, it's permission.

Ordering horses in stalls like letters, ordering chickens in houses. But they learned that from their neighbors, their grandfathers, all of whom cite, vaguely, some written down words, or, at least, oft repeated. That is their permission if/when pressed. "The Bible gave dominion," or "kill two birds with one stone," or "there's more than one way to skin a cat." Giving men permission to eat the world. Eating each letter by writing it down. Eating me with my name, the word "girl," which has a silly taste and is easy to bite, like soft cake, the kind you don't remember you even ate and have to eat something else afterward, something real.

My father used words for permission, like kidnapping something into his sack, loosed from their natural fates like pulled from a mother, or off a tree, then sold to the money men who are liars like my father, and explained by the science men and the religion men, all natural all true all right.

But, just because you can name something or add two rocks together, does not make it the correct conclusion or fate for those things. Because just as easily—in fact, looking at other species—much more easily, naturally, are things never named, never added.

Meanwhile, I take walks in the field in the bitter wind with no teacher and poor sight, with this girl notion that any killing is primordial wrong—like cracking open a cocoon before it's been finished. A thunder wrong, an earthquake wrong. A ruin, an invisible puncture to space. That there exists a universal standard against killing. Tim would say that is no guarantee, and not to put my girly morals on him. Tim says it is easier to ask forgiveness than to ask permission.

Why wouldn't it be a person's goal not to hurt anybody? Tim says the world is meant for the big fish to eat the little fish and the bigger fish still to eat the less big fish and finally for the man to eat any size fish he wants. Even though he doesn't have to do it to survive. Since a man can pick whether to be an herbivore or a killing man, a scavenger or a killing man. Just like when he gets mad, he gets to choose whether or not to kill who he's mad at. And when a lot of men get mad together, they have to choose whether to make a war and start killing each other.

That saying I always heard toward women, but men are the ones with idle hands as far as I can see. Listening to each other's words, looking for bad permissions. Women always busy with babies and lunches and suppers.

I want to get back behind the words and the stories and the cities to find the other parts of the world, to find if there is anything else, anything good. To find the place before a word, to see if there is also something kind or caring or selfless.

Before language led to the resolution of these civilizations, Tim's garage, the city. Before I trusted any person's words.

Where, after a rain, puff balls rise up out of the yard like loaves of bread. And no man knew, and no man says, and no man knows. A girl's world. Like the way the lightning bugs answer the stars.

The moon is my question, my doubt, my hope. Hanging impossibly in the sky. I feel better that it is up there, and men didn't have anything to do with it. White and strange. A boy could never understand how it hangs like magic.

And all of the stories and explanations about god and math and history is a man with human eyes trying to make everything into a road or a house. The fish, the deer, the turkey vultures do not need either and so, for them, the world must be a completely different place, have a different feel. Like emphasizing another syllable. And the moon up there floats like the light behind all of our eyes.

In the field with L, sometimes I think I've gotten behind a word like sighing or sleeping. Behind the narration of all things that happen, behind the town, behind my father's fields and his old farmhouse, behind Tim's place and Metzger's.

And there is still killing and meanness, the building and the breaking that the words remembered, memorialized. But there is also something, some sweetness that sits with L and with me, that no one ever named.

*   *   *

I've seen horses broken. My father and Tim say it's life. As if it were an involuntary act to break horses. They make it true, force it.

Science and the hard, cold fist of the monied world. This cannot be the order of things. I want to make something else true, show this place that kindness can survive, that this is not my father's terrible world.

Tear down the deer stands, kiss the cats, help the horses, move the turtles, make something else true.

THIRTY-EIGHT

My mother says that when she was a girl, she dreamt of being carried away by a giant, a slightly damaged ogre. A gentle oaf that only she could tame. She would walk through the fields and sing: *Well the big baboon by the light of the moon fell in love with the pretty maid and every night in the manilla moonlight across the bay he'd wade. Well he loved to kiss his pretty little miss in the shade of a bamboo tree and every night in the manilla moonlight it sounded like this to me…boom boom kiss kiss boom boom kiss kiss boom boom badeeadeeayyyyy.*

I've been liked by a handful of human boys, straight-toothed and laundry-clean. Sometimes even watching out for my physical safety in crowds or while walking on uneven ground, especially since my mother taught me how to achieve thinness.

I've been liked by boys who hunt and smile a lot and had braces and pay you positive attention if you are a human. Dressed in dirty camouflage, with huge trucks, messy hair, and then these alien-straight teeth from an orthodontics boom in the eighties and nineties. They have bad grammar, but they graduated with degrees from Ivy Tech or Indiana University satellite campuses, or did at least two years.

They wave and limp and smell familiar like a school desk. Woodsmoke and beer. The friendliest butchers, all rosy cheeks and thoughtful questions about my family and my work.

They probably wouldn't kill me. Just creatures on four legs. They learned to observe the difference on public school workbook pages. Four is different from two. Two is like a uniform. They learned in public school that killing me could have consequences. As opposed to all other creatures. I even liked some of those boys back before the first time I saw them kill frogs on the playground, or deer in the field.

And now, my belief in the good is the good.

In this place, romance is the dream of a fool. It makes a fool out of a woman.

That taste of acceptance. A single drop on the tongue. My father killed chickens for a living, and my mother wanted his love and attention. Sometimes he used his bare hands, and still she wanted it.

My mother says that loving the cats, and me, and L, has made her wise. Loving us has saved her from the world of men.

My mother points out dark holes on our farm. Overgrown and dangerous, smooth metal brown bars running the length of them. "Never go down there," she says. "I won't tell you what your father used to use them for. It is too terrible."

She walks me around the rotting chicken houses.

"I was so kind to him, your father. I fed him and nursed him out of sickness and once he felt better, he did such horrible things." My mother still gets tears talking about it, what he did, to the chickens, the deer.

My mother says, "It is alright to feel a mother's love. Just do not love those men. The ones who drag dogs by their necks, who build and kill and spit. Love someone who knows suffering. Love someone who deserves it."

I hide with L under blankets, having his days with him, long and quiet. We watch the men build roads and then work on them, put together cars and drive them. We are still. It is easy. I choose L, my mother, the cats. They'd never keep anything in a cage.

If you feel like you have some kind of tolerance for killing men, if you defend them on ethnic grounds or religious, look into the eyes of a dancing horse they broke, and you won't have it anymore.

I picture Tim and the dancing horse and decide I am done. Enough.

THIRTY-NINE

My mother has been happy lately. She found some videos that teach her how to pretend that everything cruel will eventually dissolve five hundred, a thousand years from now.

My mother says, when I get too sad, I should try to visualize what this land will be someday. The cows resting without the neon tags through their ears, the pigs getting to live their whole lives. She says to try to imagine the quiet of another, kinder place, and to try to believe that it will come.

I look out the back window. It's been raining. All the leaves and brush. Young groundhogs sit and chew with the daylight on their backs.

Still, since I was a child, worrying about the chickens and the cows and the mice that the cats caught, their deaths have sat on me, like Mary's death sat on her when she forced me to go to Sunday school and they told us even the hairs on our heads were numbered. Let alone our days. And on that glory terrible day, Mary would be proved right and she and Jesus together would decide what to do with us.

FORTY

My mother says that life is not other people. Never mind all of that between-the-lines that exists in talk and writing. It's very freeing, she says.

She says that I can write down whatever I want, but it won't change the fact that the world is not a human being. It is not united under a common logic, like the same kind of logic that underlies Chicago or New York City. It'd be nice for the men if that were the case, she says. All of the outside species like a classroom full of children who keep failing at infrastructure.

But, she says, the alive world is a suspension of air and insects, knit together by fields and woods. The world is out-side, buzzing and grunting. Often too cold for a human's skin, maybe not a dog's or a bear's, though. Sometimes too hot, although fine for snakes and lizards. She says the real day outside slides and halts.

She says that we human people invent language and truth—which are one in the same—and upon this, men built cities, channeling death into rivers, sending it north-ward, southward.

FORTY-ONE

In the fall, in rural Indiana, if you have any goodness at all in you, you drive real slow. My mother says good people get in a hurry, but that is no excuse. Deer are running for their lives and cross the roads like they're made of ice. Farmers are closing up their fields, rolling up hay bales like spooled thread. The hay bales hold the moonlight the way the tops of corn plants hold the setting sun a few extra seconds after it sets. The fields are full of spun hay and black cows. Farmers' objects. Tim puts his hands on his hips and looks out over them both like they equal each other. Takes a breath about arranging them the way you might over a plate of food put in front of you at a restaurant.

There are men who write about living an ethos of kindness and empathy to all of mankind. The reasoning being that everyone is doing their best. I am thinking this as Tim is driving his tractor in perfect rectangles around the farm, cutting hay. But, if I support Tim, where does that put me in relation to the deer, allegiance-wise? Even when I am nice to Tim, giving him a pitying smile, it may give him a little extra spring in his step as he does his work. His work being all the deer's hell.

The men who write about being nicer might suggest that if Tim feels better about himself, it may increase the chances he, down the line, stops and realizes the error of his ways regarding deer. But, I know Tim and if he had more money, he'd just buy a better bow.

FORTY-TWO

On fall afternoons, the fields become light and dry and the sky gets heavy like a stormy sea.

Tim comes over early evening. Mom is too friendly, and I am too friendly. We drink lukewarm beer from dusty cans. Mom drinks three and falls asleep, and I am left alone with him.

He says they're getting together a group of them. A militia. He just wanted to let me know. Gary came up with the idea, and the boys living on Harmon's old farm got a cannon, so now they have two. It's not thunder I'm hearing, they've been setting it off for practice. I know, I say.

He says Gary told him to come over and to say on behalf of the militia, they don't see why they can't hunt in our field. They are allowed to hunt on every other farm here, he says. They are good and want to protect us, and in exchange, telling them they can hunt on our farm without stirring up trouble is the least we can do. And really, they could do it anyway except they believe in personal property, which is nice of them compared to Arabs.

Tim doesn't wait for me to respond. He goes right into asking about Jay. Says he hasn't seen his fancy car around for a while. Yeah, I say.

I was too nice to Tim after Mary died. He believes I will eventually agree to marry him, and this is the only reason Gary and the other hunting men have mostly stayed off of our land until now.

Tim stands up and says that he wants to show me the meet-up place for the new militia, and I don't feel like I can tell him no. He says we can take a shortcut through my mother's field. The sun has set, and I follow him past where the deer, who I mistook for my mother, became invisible into the tall, dense corn last summer, past the muskrat's lake. Everything harvested, cut down, and flat now, and bare.

We come up on the old house that Mrs. Longyear used to own until she died and now it's waiting for auction. No one is farming it, so tall dry weeds stand all through the field. The skeletons of Queen Anne's lace to my chest.

We approach what looks like a boys' camp. Gun racks. Big guns, not just rifles, but guns from movies, and the two cannons, and deer mannequins, and human mannequins. Like walking onto an old battlefield, I've come into a killing man's mind. My father's. And I can picture the killing men driving straight there after work. Their excitement, like they could make something true, like they had something.

With Tim at the militia house, I am hit by an intense feeling of helplessness. I realize, in his life, forever, it will be up to him—something inside of him—to stop from hitting and punching and killing as many of us as he feels inclined to. Speaking my mind could anger him. And what would stop him from one night remembering what I said and beating me up like a man in a bar, or shooting me like a wild deer?

Feels thin as a hair, whatever is in a killing man to stop when the whole world seems holding its breath, preparing for him to do it.

In my life, I've stopped some boys from touching snakes, frogs, large worms, possums, raccoons, a deer. But, I've mostly failed. I can't write down all of my stories. I am too tired, and they are too terrible. I'll just say that if you lived out here in the place where horses are broken and cows are destroyed, and baby chickens bought in 24 cases like beer, you could never really love or trust another human person again, not all the way.

The men, like my father, who see war everywhere, who shoot holes through flesh ears with the sun glowing through them. You will never trust them. Men who will become old men.

And how I betray the cows, the deer, the horses, by being friendly to Tim. By using my imagination to pretend away the bad, killing things he does.

*   *   *

There is no way out of some situations, like the existence of the buildings and the city. Once a militia man walks into a room, it is his room, there is war in the room, and the rest of us have to figure out how to handle it. He becomes a building and we are just people, just the air.

Sometimes there is no going back. There is no return. It is not detectable by science, but my belly churns like a nightmare, a black nest. Like a bad train's coming soon, and fast.

FORTY-THREE

Do you want to be there at the beginning of human civ-ilization? Do you want to witness it? It cycles over and over again, and builds layers over itself, discs. If you could have been with us at the militia camp, I think you would see. How it all starts over.

Civilization is recreated every morning as the killing men swing their legs out of beds. It wakes up with the will or routine habits of men waking up.

Who they are, the conquerors in each generation, is not important. They are like the faces of house guests, names in a registry, numbers, years, the exact temperatures for record highs and record lows marked down in farmers' almanacs.

Rural women know who plants the seeds of war. But they will kill us if we tell you. So we will never say. No one listens to rural women, anyway.

Tim and I are alone in the yard behind the militia house. It is quiet and I am trying to work up the courage to tell him that I think we should just be friends, and that I plan to take care of my mother just like she did with Mary, and then be alone with the cats forever. And, for a minute, I feel warm thinking of my mother and our home and the cats. Cotton and sweetness and help and sleep.

But then, Tim tries to kiss me, and I pull away. He looks upset and I can't get anything to come out of my mouth. He takes a breath and says his intentions are good. He says my name, and then he asks me to marry him. He says it's time for me to decide.

I tell him no. I just say no, I'm sorry, and then I stand up and run into the dark. And as I run, the dry weeds whip against my legs, and I feel heavier and sicker until I realize I have gotten my mother and myself in trouble now. Serious. Like school or law or money.

Don't do that. Those men are dangerous in their trucks. They end lives with the palms of their hands and their fingers. They live in a world of objects and surfaces—big, small, soft, hard—not bodies and souls. Now you listen to me. Now, I mean it.

FORTY-FOUR

Soon after I run home, Tim comes walking up with his typical belly, but I see something else now. I see the deer folded up under his skin, in his abdomen. Dead. Floating. Just their deaths, the fact of their deaths done.

Tim is different now at our house. He is agitated, angry, irritated at the sight of me. First the coyotes, then the tiles and the deer stands, not accepting him was the last straw. Without looking at me, he says to my mother, who was awakened by his too-loud knock, that the militia will be needing to use our field, and he'll be telling Gary and the boys to go ahead. He says we are on our own.

In this world of men on top of land, Tim is a killing man with horse brides, who lives surrounded by other men in their fields with their horse brides and cow brides. At night, they visit each other and swallow dark fluids from cloudy glasses as the horse brides shift their weight and stare through the fence at the cow brides through the dark. The cows show the whites of their eyes at the slightest sound or movement near the houses with the men inside, with their orange-yellow lights that make the flies turn true black in contrast, like toys or candy. Oh, to be a fly, too small for men to catch, to contain. Together, we all wait for the kind sun to come back.

FORTY-FIVE

Tonight, late into the night, there are gunshots, explosions on our property, and I am blind behind the still-dark field. Wondering what will happen. Because I won't do anything back. Like the deer Tim kills, I don't use guns. I don't shoot. I am a fish, and Tim is a fisherman. At least the deer try to run—I don't even run. Where would I go?

A pickup truck comes down our lane at 4 a.m. and idles in the gravel for twenty minutes. Mom and I wake up and hide against the wall under the window. I pull my shirt down over my folded legs and we wait for three hours for the sun to come up.

We crouch like rabbits and the sun rises and the sky blooms. A blue dome. Light and strange. We, each with hearts soft as the inside of your cheek. Quiet and begging. Let. Us. Live.

FORTY-SIX

In the morning, we call the deputy sheriff about the men coming onto our property, and he says they'd have to still be there when the deputy arrives in order for them to do anything about it. But we know that Gary's deputy sheriff nephew will call Gary as soon we call him, and the boys will pack up and be gone long before the deputy comes. And, the deputy will come to the door and act put out at making the trip. Why don't we just let them do what they need to do? We silly irritating things. He will warn us that we will look back and be sorry for feeling so upset and angry. Like how you feel bad in the morning when you eat all of the peanut butter at night.

I don't know what will become of us. Gary's militia is silly, but Gary gets drunk and Gary gets mad, and they have enough guns to wipe out all of Claypool if they decided to. And now, we have become something for him to focus his attention on. We have become targets. Two women trying to keep men off of land. A kind of resistance Gary considers offensive and unpatriotic.

With Tim's feelings hurt, and Gary over at night idling his truck like saying, "here kitty, kitty." Things have changed. We are finally their targets, alone in the country with them with no witnesses. I put up five "no trespassing" signs around the perimeter of the farm and Gary tore them down the same day.

My mother and I look at each other. She says it will just have to blow over. She says if we lie low, they will run out of energy for the anger and it will lighten. Still, we wake for work and feel sick in the pits of our stomachs all day, unraveled in indefinable, invisible ways. We do not have the means to leave, and we could never leave the cats. There is nowhere to go. Just here. Just this. More of this. Them. Faster and meaner, now. And we are small fish. Now who will hold back the tiny sharp men always on the horizon line like tin?

FORTY-SEVEN

As a girl on my father's farm, I imagined that I would become a hero. Put on a ski mask and rescue armfuls of chickens. Break laws for sake of life and death—they aren't real like death is real, they are just laws some human people came up with, after all.

I would have never guessed that a place to hide everyone would be the most important thing I would not have. So simple. Sneak the chickens out of the pens, the cows and pigs, Tim's underfed horses—where would I put them? How would I keep them secret and pay for their care?

I could never have imagined that in a world with this sky, with sleep and stars and woods and more other species than we have numbers for, it would come down to what Tim thinks of me, or Gary. That this would determine safety for us, for L, for the cats.

The killing men play it perfectly black—a threat so cold it feels familiar like that mystical threat of death we always have on us. The killing men, in their willingness to make death happen right then, right there, trick us into thinking they know something more about it, something secret, but it is like fool's gold. They are not gods of men or natural predators,

they have a genetic disorder. They were born without the ability to feel the pull of compassion or the ache of connection,
like how Tim's cousin was born without some of her fingers
and toes.

Still, they are dangerous because the rest of us haven't figured out what to do with them. They become our leaders. They
run roughshod. They make themselves agents, boy-agents.
A hundred thousand years of them placing their whole arms
inside someone else's body. In their presence, my mother and
I, the deer, the rabbits, the cows, pigs, chickens, are nothing
but daft mercy. Breathing in and out.

Every night now, I am afraid men will kill my mother
and me, jimmy open the back door and stomp down the hall-
way to where we sleep. Shoot us with a rifle or a machine
gun from Walmart, like the kind they use in the fields in the
mornings and evenings. All day on weekends. We, like the
cows and the deer and everything else, are at their mercy.
I wake up all night and check the locks until 5 a.m. when
I figure they would have come by now and then let myself
sleep until the alarm.

FORTY-EIGHT

A week later, I wake up in the middle of the night to the sound of men talking. And I hear gunshots close, an engine pulling away.

In the morning, my mother and I find a bullet hole in our tiny basement window that sits almost level with the ground.

I don't know if it was intentional—the boys drive around to shine lights and shoot at night animals—or whether it was meant to threaten us. At the very least, it proves that the killing men are coming onto the property. Hunting in our fields. The deer are not safe even on these eighty acres. I ask my mother what she thinks we should do. She runs her fingers over the bullet hole and does not say a word.

FORTY-NINE

I have bad visions. Mostly at night, but anytime I let my mind a little loose. Blood I can't stop, sudden breathlessness, a field of tiny creatures floating up to the sky. Too many for me to catch, or I keep missing.

In this place of machines and guns, held together by science and money, dissolving the skin of every living thing, full of lead and mercury and the dirty hands of working men, worry is the anti-structure. Heavy worry. All of that negative space heaped upon me like displaced gravity after all of men's impossible flying, building.

My world is crystalline, fragile. L's life is like a cluster of a thousand tiny white moths, wings thinner than paper. I surround him with my worry, like an energy field, to try and protect him against bullets and cars and anything else the men might decide to do.

My mother used to follow around my father like an insect, a bug, nagging, warning, trying to control, to limit, even a little, his carelessness. He was always hurting things, breaking them. "Please, be careful, John. Be careful now, John. See them under there? Now wait. Tell me what you're planning to cut. Let me check to make sure the cats are in. Don't open that door! What if you don't see the newborn rabbits and run them over with your tractor?"

For my mother to watch what my father was doing and then to worry, to nag it into something even just a little more cautious, more careful, would make my father very angry, as if it seemed incorrectly inconvenient to him. The air suddenly much too thick with considerations and he couldn't have his speed. My mother's words and concerns like thick seaweed, clinging vines.

Now that my father is gone, my mother and I can protect and take care of L and the cats. Their lives are delicate and precious as pulled glass. Still, the men fire shots near the house and put their paint-covered hands in our water so that it looks milky and makes us get headaches after dinner.

We hide L and the cats in our house, behind this line of trees. And then the rain. And a distant pop pop.

My mother shakes her head at the sound of the guns. She looks at the cats and says, "You have to help one at a time. All it takes is one man to explode a bomb, a few trucks to destroy a grass field. Death and destruction come so easy, so quick, like water rushing, a flood."

"And helping takes so much longer. I wish I would have known," she says. "That the killing men make large-scale change toward destruction, in grand swift motions, waving their arms over their heads. But, alive things must be helped one at a time. And usually you don't even know you've helped. It's invisible. This is what helping is. Nothing quantifiable in response to the invention of quantifiable things, like men's money and men's objects."

FIFTY

They say some time many years ago, humans changed from scavengers to hunters. But I did not change, or my mother. We are still the kind of human who does not kill animals, who only scavenges for survival like the long black turkey vultures I love, the turkey vultures who I hope will take me away when I die, and then sit on top of my father's old barn and open their wings to feel the sun.

Men said they turned into hunters, but maybe they did not. We did not. And so maybe they did not. Have they really become something else? Tim, the neighbor boys and their militia—are they the hunters with spears on cave walls? Maybe the men drew pictures of those things on the walls of caves to ask themselves for, and simultaneously, grant themselves permission to do the killing, to make the days feel simpler, easier, faster. Because the idea mind is a man's membranous maker, and whenever he checks, it is always a yes.

Or, maybe the women drew those stick figures in caves because watching the men killing the animals felt as wrong and as bad to them as it feels to my mother and me. Maybe they felt helpless against it, so they marked it down like a record, leaving it for the future to stop it, or calling out to some bigger, stronger, kinder power to help.

Men split the world. But no one can remember exactly how they did it, so, now a world split, and a human history that has become as mysterious as that of the planet. But, I know a man in a way one could never know the complexities of an earth. I know his brain and his eye and his sounds.

And as far as I can tell, the killing men are scavengers with fathers who stumble upon the convenience of enslavement and killing like fire, like a coin in the street. To take. To take without telling, then to hide it somewhere and sing a vibrato survival into the dusk. Unscrupulous opportunists gone mad with permissions. Giddy for repeatable outcomes. Confusing predictability with aggression, with the physics of destruction. Creatures, now, who I am wise not to anger.

So, what are the rest of us? What am I? Containers of cruel deeds, like timekeepers, to keep the men from destroying it all in one unbound generation?

I look out the back window.

My life is a story with the killing men as narrators.

What are they doing out the window? Shooting their guns out into the night and out into the morning. My mother says shame on them.

My mother says that the story of a history is always inaccurate. It is the act of a human trying to make a line out of nothing. Trying to make reasons out of finished things, outcomes. You cannot trust stories, because the truth is, my mother says, nobody really knows, and how dare they. The world full of everything going on at once.

What is it to be good? To decide that if something is unkind, it is the same as being structurally unsound. And all that surrounds you is the languageless outdoors.

FIFTY-ONE

It is November. The air is not clean and sweet. Many different kinds of smokes. Men burning their garbage instead of paying to have it sent to the Stafford family's land off 800 South where the landfill is. Men burning things no one is supposed to burn, things that should never have been invented. Making green smoke. Men smoking their kills in plastic sheds they bought at Big R's or out of the garden center at Walmart. The ethanol plant. Dalton's and Donnelley's.

Men fill up our field now. They sit in trees. They lie on their stomachs on the ground. They stand on rocks. In between rows of dry corn, they stand straight as statues. Some are still, and some are restless. They are waiting for things to move. Outside things. Things in the outside, our outside. Anything. And then, they shoot. Poppoppoppoppop.

What do you do with a killing man, a conqueror?

Do you fight back? Try to conquer the field yourself to protect it from being conquered by a conqueror? Do you hide like a rabbit? Run like a deer? Be a surrenderer? An angry, yelling surrenderer or a quiet one who just knows inside she's surrendered?

They wanted the land to farm it, to hunt all of the wild living things upon it. And they took it. We have no recourse. Gary and the neighbor boys park their trucks across the field at Tim's and walk over, so the deputy sheriff says he doesn't see them. Most of the time, my mother and I hide in the house. Like rabbits in a warren, the deer in the woods. And when we do come outside, we are afraid not to smile, not to lie.

All hours of the day and night. Worse on weekends.

Men in our fields now. Filling them up.

FIFTY-TWO

This morning, my mother says that she thinks that maybe being dead isn't so bad. "I mean, look at what men can do, how they can cause it so easily," she says. "Maybe it's not so bad. It would be too mean if it were terrible—unrealistically mean."

She says, maybe death is even better than life, feels good. And that all of this knocking each other into and out of it is not much more than bumping into someone on the sidewalk, temporarily stepping into their personal space. Seeing Mary enter death made her think about it.

"Plus," my mother says, "we've already been through it once. Before we were born we didn't exist and it couldn't have been that bad. So we should not be scared about not existing again one day."

Still, at night, my mother and I bolt the doors and L, the cats, my mother, and I try to sleep. We keep a security light on as a signal we learned in the world of men, like fences. The light, a signal, like a little cloud of words hovering above the house in the moonlight, and in the fog: Please don't. Please no.

FIFTY-THREE

It is late evening. Unseasonably warm for late fall, and not many gunshots tonight. The bats are waking up and darting around the purple sky.

The young pregnant calico cat hasn't been to the porch for a couple of days. She is sick, and my mother has been watching for her, going every few hours to their meeting place with a plate of food.

My mother thinks she hears the cat crying from the field, just across the yard. She prepares another plate of food, and puts on her coat, and says she'll be right back, and walks out into the yard.

A shot. Close. I run out and my mother is lying on the ground. She has become a dark shape in the low light, a single hay bale if I didn't know better.

Tim comes running up holding his rifle halfway up like a baseball bat. All in camouflage.

I am holding my mother, but she is gone. Tim is a good shot on account of all of his practice.

"Oh my god," he says. "I thought she was a deer. I was sure."

Pause.

"I'm so sorry," he says. He has his hand on his face. "Oh god," he says. He takes out his phone to call the ambulance.

I am holding my mother, but she is gone. Tim is a good shot.

Faster than the geese startle up off the lake, she is gone. Like after a rain.

FIFTY-FOUR

Sometimes the moon is high and crisp and tight and dense like a jewel, and sometimes it is wide and soft and loose and thin at the horizon, and that is how I have begun to feel. I am uncoiling, becoming less taut, slower.

It is heavy to carry myself across the half-flooded yard. The sky not silver like my mother tried to call it—"Another silver day!"—but the color of the off side of steel, as opposed to the shine side. The work side, the slop side.

Heavy to carry my body to pick up L's ball and brush off the mud and watch him splash across the yard to plop it into another half-water-filled hole.

I don't have that thing anymore, that thing that carries a person through the world of people: ambition, delusion, allegiance to a story when a story is a hat that'd look silly on anything but a human person in a world full of everything all happening at once, full of species far outnumbering just this human one.

Living our lives with L, the cats, the rabbits, and the deer—my mother and I touched something, a tiny thing. Tiny as the six red petals in the center of Queen Anne's lace. I think we touched the texture of a mystery of existence before a human person tried to net it in stories and roads, words and infrastructure. We lived in a world in which a human is equal to a cow, and to a cat, and to a moth. All of us alive together. All of our lives the same size, like a field of lightning bugs.

My mother once said that we had become unmoored from the human world. And, once you are unmoored, you will no longer have the human people's help forgetting death. And you won't have their permissions for taking things or killing things. Their old stories will become thinner and thinner, then air. Flimsy as a memory, the frail, filmy material of a thought.

And then you might become very sad, seeing the killing men ride invisible permissions like wild horses they caught and broke, and you also might become very tired. Sleepy. Like fog over still water. Left only with that tiny thing that wakes the cats in the morning, same thing that makes the cows wake and watch, the rabbits wake and run. Then, it's just up to you why we're here and what all of this means. Then you're in it with the frogs and the flies, mosquitos and everybody else.

All of this air. Temperature, do you love me? Do I belong here?

The alive world doesn't make any sense. That might be our problem—a human person's. That things can be built, take on a sense of forward motion, arranged into rows like a human person's brain likes—makes things more comfortable like words, stories. We like rows, so we make them. Before us, there were no rows.

The alive world is luck or chaos or suffering or death. And where do I put all of my grief? My love? The killing men riding around killing everything, and the women either helping or trying not to.

My mother is gone. And one day I will go. And everyone I love. These easy days will devolve back into nonsense, before a human person's brain arranged it.

In the meantime, I choose to tell myself a story about a logic of kindness and gentleness, and try to hold it in my mind as long as I can, like an image, a memory, a dream. Like the way the turkey vultures float on currents of air without moving their wings. As long as they can hold it.

* * *

There are two different kinds of floating. Floating like the men do in their planes and machines, and floating like the moon.

In the late evening, I sit in the grass with L, and stare at the old machinery in the barnyard now, mercifully, dormant and left to the rabbits, deer, and vultures. Brake dust and cast metal details I wonder if anyone but L and I have ever noticed. Because when you slow down here, this great anxiety catches up to you. That you do not understand the outdoors. That the power could go off. That men swear that life is a periodic table, and an explosion, and a place for money to evolve and become a future of skyscrapers and computer logic, but somehow your body is still here carrying an outdoorsy death in it. Out of place and sticking to you. Pure unsolvable. You know how, once an element is listed on the periodic table, it is the definition of solved, clear, defined? Death is everything that element is not. Not listed, not categorized, not filed. Like the view from an insect's eye.

We, modern humans in the world of men, carry sense and order around on our bodies like gaudy conchs or snails. Withdrawing into them, like into a dream.

In the outside, everything is naked. Death feels close. And the hawks take everybody's babies in the day. The owls take them at night, like devils. My mother used to say it's a solemn thing—our lives out here alone with this other world, this born world. To see the baby rabbits, the wildness of life, the uncertainty. Thirty years is a lucky-long life in this world.

I am comforted by my mother's idea that death must not be terrible, just strange like outer space. But, inside, all of my love pushes against my stomach and my chest, like the spring pushes water across the field, like a heart pushes blood. Wishing it could push away death, so that L, the cats, my mother and I, could stay together forever in a perfect suspension of sweetness, attachment, and care.

FIFTY-FIVE

Tim went to jail for four months. They called it negligent homicide. So strange that there is suddenly a language for what he has done to deer and raccoons and coyotes for all these years. Story of this place, my mother would say.

Once he got back, he, in his guilt, promised to stop hunting. He keeps the killing men off of the land now. I don't see much of Gary anymore. Every once in a while, I catch sight of him driving slow past the house, staring from his truck on the road.

Tim comes over every day or two, to mow or to unload litter for the cats, or to carry bags to the dumpster.

He looks at me, and by extension the cats, with a sense of fear. He is clumsily attentive. An unpracticed careful, slow.

Before he leaves, he asks me how I am doing. He asks what he can do. If I need money or anything. He says the deer walk right through his field now, sometimes even get close to his house and he just leaves them be. Even if their antlers are big.

At night, I sit where my mother was. I listen for her. I wonder if she is a salamander now or a tadpole, or a mayfly. She could be a deer herself, a fawn, maybe. And maybe she will get to keep her mother this year, without Tim hunting.

My mother once said, when I asked her if she was okay after Mary died, that she knew that she was not ever alone in her grief.

She said, when you grieve, look around these fields. See the mother cats who lose their kittens, the fawns who lose their mothers. You always have someone nearby who has survived losing someone they loved, to lead you into the field, to move you back into the day until you can do it again yourself.

*   *   *

The pregnant calico cat who my mother was feeding came to the front door the morning after my mother died. It was cold, and I coaxed her into the house. She cautiously agreed to come in. She ate and slept for three days, and then she lost her kittens. She was too sick, and none of them survived.

I am learning from her how to continue. We lie on the warm wood floor across the room from each other, and the light changes and the air, and we sleep and eat, and the experience of our losses has become invisible as the air, but it is on us, like age. But, we are not alone.

I watch Tim out the window with his axe. I can see his breath in the cold, spring air. He is building a new ramp for the calico cat, who is stronger now, and who sleeps near me in my mother's room. The ramp goes out my mother's window and leads to a big field Tim has fenced in for her, so that when it gets warmer, she'll be able to come and go as she pleases. He was careful to choose small enough chain link that she would not get her paw stuck if she tried to reach through the fence.

FIFTY-SIX

It is summer. I have been taking walks in the warm evenings. The black horse in Tim's field watches me walk up the driveway and turn onto the road. Twilight. No cars. She watches me walk along the road toward her and when I get next to the fence, she starts to walk alongside me. I walk faster and she walks faster. I run, and she runs, and we are head to head and just flying in the lavender air! And then she comes to the end of her fence, and stops. And so I turn around, and then she turns around, and we race back the length of her fence the other way, and I laugh and laugh. She watches me walk back down the road to the house. I check over my shoulder and see her smaller and smaller, black standing and watching from Tim's field.

On my way back to the house, I lift a turtle from the middle of the road, the road still hot from the sun that's just set. It has the smell of oil and bitter, alkaline gravel. And, for a moment, the world is not all bad. For a moment, that turtle lives in a world my father would swear doesn't exist. Anomalous, Jay would say, like my life with L and the cats. But that turtle is lifted from his or her place of danger and carried carefully across and wished well. By some oaf like me. Big and lumbering luck.

Tonight, I do what my mother taught me, to picture the fields like I've wished them. I practice her imagining. I imagine that the horses are not broken, and that the llamas are not displaced, that the cows get to have their whole lives. And my wishes, my hope, my imagining, is the stream when there no longer exists a stream. The moonlight past where moonlight is visible. The unwillingness to hurt, or to kill anything.

My life, like my mother's, is a whisper, like the blue doves who live secretly in green caves, like things that glow underwater where you will never find. So, if you stumble upon some creature late at night when you should be sleeping, it could be my hope stretching its legs. And you will probably not find it twice.

But I hope that from a world that gives us sleep, death is not just absence, suffering has its limit, and that we are suspended in something that we can never be lost from. No matter how mean the killing men are, I hope that all of us, the deer, the rabbits, the cats, my mother, are being born and dying within a kind of air it is impossible to become lost from. Outside, my hope stands still in the field, like a deer in the moonlight.

And I have written all of this down only to remember, and to put on some kind of record, that some of us do not live in the world of the killing men, and cannot stand it. When I die, like my mother, I will not go to heaven or to hell. I will go where the sticky-eyed kittens go, the cows, the deer, and all the rest of us creatures who live here, in the field that used to be a woods.

END